Grace and Mercy

7 Short Stories of
God's Grace and Mercy over
the Lives of 7 Women

Yasmina Delacruz-Bailey

ISBN 979-8-88943-995-0 (paperback)
ISBN 979-8-88943-996-7 (digital)

Copyright © 2023 by Yasmina Delacruz-Bailey

All rights reserved. No part of this publication may be reproduced, distributed, or transmitted in any form or by any means, including photocopying, recording, or other electronic or mechanical methods without the prior written permission of the publisher. For permission requests, solicit the publisher via the address below.

Christian Faith Publishing
832 Park Avenue
Meadville, PA 16335
www.christianfaithpublishing.com

Printed in the United States of America

Contents

Preface v
Acknowledgments vii
I: Hope 1
    Scripture Reflections 8
    Let Us Pray 10
II: Joy 11
    Scripture Reflections 20
    Let Us Pray 23
III: Faith 24
    Scripture Reflections 33
    Let Us Pray 35
IV: Patience 36
    Scripture Reflections 44
    Let Us Pray 46
V: Temperance 47
    Scripture Reflections 53
    Let Us Pray 55
VI: Justice 56
    Scripture Reflections 62
    Let Us Pray 64
VII: Love 65
    Scripture Reflections 75
    Let Us Pray 77
The Lord's Prayer 79

Preface

Grace encompasses various meanings, including favor, goodwill, kindness, and approval. It's also characterized as unearned, divine assistance granted to humans for their spiritual renewal or sanctification. Additionally, it is regarded as a virtuous quality originating from God. In the Bible, grace is described as God's choice to bless us, His kindness towards us, His generous and undeserved favor, and His spiritual blessings upon our lives. Ephesians 2:8-9 (NIV) says "For it is by grace you have been saved, through faith— and this is not from yourselves, it is the gift of God— not by works, so that no one can boast."

As sinners, none of us deserve grace, but God is the epitome of grace, offering unconditional love. Regardless of our actions, His love remains unwavering. He continues to be good to us, favoring us even when we doubt, fear, hate, or sin. His grace persists, a testament to His boundless love.

Mercy is defined as compassion or forgiveness shown toward someone whom it is within one's power to harm or punish. It is also defined as lenient or compassionate treatment. The Bible defines mercy as giving forgiveness or withholding punishment.

We receive God's grace and mercy because he loves us. God is a compassionate and forgiving God, who keeps no record of our wrongs. Lamentations 3:22–23 (KJV) says "It is of the LORD's mercies that we are not consumed, Because his compassions fail not. They are new every morning: Great is thy faithfulness."

God's grace and mercy are a constant presence in our lives, provided to us each day. The key lies in recognizing and acknowledging these gifts. Often, we overlook the fact that without His grace and mercy, our mornings wouldn't begin. Each day offers fresh opportunities – chances to make amends, opportunities to praise Him for His boundless love. Unfortunately, we sometimes fail to grasp this, taking it all for granted. We neglect to give Him the glory He deserves for His grace and mercy. There are moments when we mistakenly believe it was solely our own efforts that carried us through, or we question whether we truly deserve His blessings. Regardless of our thoughts, God continues to bestow His grace and mercy upon us, sustaining us with the very breath we need to live.

In 'Grace and Mercy: 7 Short Stories,' you'll immerse yourself in the lives of seven fictional characters, each inspired by a different real woman, myself included. Each character's story is unique and unrelated to the others in the book. Although these stories aren't exact replicas of real events, they closely mirror the lives of those who inspired them. These stories remind us that we all have our own unique journeys, and any one of these women could be you. Through it all, God's grace and mercy shine brightly in our lives every day. Let's always remember to give Him the glory!

Acknowledgments

After countless nights, procrastination, prayers, sermons, reading, and subliminal messages, I heard the voice. I want to, first and foremost, thank my Almighty Lord and Savior, Jesus Christ, for His grace and mercy every day and for helping me get through the nights when I had writer's block.

A special thank you to my loving husband, Kevin Bailey, for his love, patience, support, and encouragement. Thank you for putting up with me burning the midnight oil to complete this book and for being my biggest cheerleader.

An extra special thanks to my babies, my children, my not-so-little boys—Jared, Josiah, and Jensen Brown—for their unconditional love and support and for always believing in me and making me a proud mom.

An extra, extra special thank you to my mom, Maria DeLaCruz, for all her prayers and love. No matter how distant we were physically, she always made her presence felt with her daily phone calls.

Thank you to my music ministry director, my sister in Christ, and my friend, Michele Rouse, for the prayers and encouragement and for always lending an ear right before church service. Singing alongside you and being in the music ministry have been life changing, and for that, I am grateful.

Thank you to my counselor/therapist, Dr. Karen Gore, for the advice and emotional support throughout the years. You have played such a vital role in my personal development, and for that, I say thank you.

Thank you to my pastor, Rev. Elvin Clayton, for your leadership, guidance, and prayers. Thank you for being such a great example of living a life of faith.

Thank you to my Walters Memorial AME Zion Church family for their support and prayers.

Thank you to my productivity coach, Lucas Hine, for the motivation to keep going and for helping me organize my calendar to get my life together and finally finish this book.

Thank you to my extended family and best friends—you all know who you are—for the inspiration and motivation. It's not over! God got us!

Thank you to my publisher and editor, Christian Faith Publishing, for your patience and your amazing work with this project.

I

Hope

Hope was the oldest of her siblings. She had five sisters and three brothers. Not all of them were from her mom and dad together. Despite her mom and dad's divorce when she was only four years old and her dad having other children in his second marriage, she was really close with all her siblings. She always felt as if she had to set an example for her brothers and sisters, and she felt the pressure every time.

She grew up in a large family surrounded by her siblings, grandparents, many uncles and aunts, innumerable cousins, and granduncles and grandaunts. She was a happy child, easy to please, and quick to laugh. To many eyes, she made a pretty picture with her bushy curls, dreamy hazel eyes, and dimpled cheeks that stunned many a looker when she smiled. Hope was the sunshine in the lives of her mom and dad. She had more than enough love than she needed. Her gentle spirit and beautiful soul endeared her to many.

She loved quite many things, as she was easy to satisfy, but dearest to her were her dolls. She cared for them with the attention and devotion of a mother. She made sure her little ones were well-fed, clean, and entertained.

Even as a child, she loved children and loved to be in their care. In her teens, she spent her afternoons babysitting for her neighbors and taking care of her siblings who lived with her and her mom. How she loved those little persons! It seemed like a long time to wait before prince charming would come to sweep her off her feet, have a home full of kids, and then live happily ever after.

There had never been any question that she would marry Johnny. They had been dating since their first year in college. His father was the pastor of the church she attended, and they both grew up singing in the church choir, performing one church activity or another. Everyone who knew them together would surely have agreed that there wasn't a better-matched pair. Johnny earned his master's in business administration while Hope received her master's in education. Nothing made her happier than teaching her sixth graders.

Hope's mom and dad had been Christians for as long as she could remember, and she grew up seeing them involved in church activities. She grew up surrounded by love, protected, and fussed over.

Johnny and Hope got married a few years after college. Their wedding was fairly big, considering the fact that they had many mutual friends from the church attend.

Their marriage got off to a good start. They were young and very much in love. Johnny nearly couldn't wait to be home with his wife every day. They were both committed to church activities. She sang in the church choir and taught a class of nine-year-old children in Sunday school while he was involved in various projects, missions, and community work.

Their home was an awesome picture of love, peace, unity, and everything one would want in a marriage and remained that way for three years before tragedy started rearing its ugly head.

They started trying for a baby in the second year of their marriage after which she got pregnant, and their joy knew no bounds. What followed, however, was unimaginable. On a cold winter night into the fourth month of her pregnancy, she woke up feeling a sharp pain in her abdomen and was filled with horror to discover bloodstains on the sheet.

"Johnny!" she cried out as she shook her husband. "Something's wrong with the baby."

Her husband jumped up, startled.

She told him again, crying, "Something's wrong. Call 911!"

Frantically, he grabbed his phone and dialed 911. Ten long minutes later, an ambulance arrived to take them to the nearest hospital. Johnny held Hope's hands throughout the journey to the hospital which seemed to be the longest ride they'd ever taken. He tried all he could to soothe her with calming words. He stroked her back with each gut-wrenching sob while his insides were churning and kept whispering words of assurance while she cried, "My baby!"

The tires screeched to a halt, and the ambulance doors were jerked open. What happened in the next few minutes was a blur, with doctors and nurses all over her as she was wheeled in by the paramedics and prepared for an emergency operation. All the while, the only words she uttered as she trembled were, "God, please save my baby," and the last thing she remembered before she zoned out was her husband's hands on the glass doors, muttering some words she couldn't hear.

When she woke up, she knew something went totally wrong. Everywhere was filled with gifts, handmade cards from her students, flowers, and chocolate. Her husband was at her bedside holding her hand in his, eyes wracked with grief, yet tender, and in that moment, she knew. Time stood still as she poured out her grief and wept for her baby—for the things that could have been, for the hope that was snatched like a dangling thread, and for a part of her that was gone. Little did she know that her troubles, like the temptation of Job, were just beginning.

Time, they say, heals all wounds, but being surrounded by people who truly care and love you speeds up the healing process.

Her students from school and their parents came by in droves to see her, bringing with them little gifts that conveyed more than a thousand words about how dear their pretty teacher was to them. Church members sent over casseroles, pies, and various homemade dishes. Her girlfriends and sisters took turns in keeping her company. Her parents came over, and her mom stayed with her while Johnny was simply the best husband anyone could have.

Nonetheless, she healed fast and became her usual cheerful self, and whatever scars remained faded as in the following year she was pregnant again. This time around, she took extreme precautions including taking a leave of absence from work the moment she discovered she was pregnant. She gave herself lots of rest and kept all her hospital appointments. She spent her days reading, tending her flowers, and coming up with a lot of ridiculous projects which were executed by her husband under her supervision.

However, on another cold winter night, tragedy struck again. She slept and dreamed that she was playing with a little girl on a beach. The little girl had big curly hair and eyes exactly like hers. She laughed as the sand tickled her feet and stretched out her hands to Hope and said, "Mama." To her mortification, the closer she moved to the child, the farther away she appeared to be. Suddenly, a violent wind gathered, the clouds turned dark, and white lightning flashes started across the sky. She screamed and made a dash for the baby without being able to see what was in front of her and woke up still screaming. She found herself in the arms of her husband, who was thoroughly shaken up and confused. A sharp glance at her nightdress confirmed her worst fears, and her heart broke all over again. "God, not again!" She wept bitterly on the way to the hospital and wouldn't be consoled.

Johnny was steeped in grief and never felt so useless in his entire life that he couldn't do anything about the situation. This time around, the ordeal was shorter than the previous one, and things weren't the same again. She had so many questions to ask God if only she could get a chance to see Him. Her prayer life became ashes of what it used to be, and churchgoing became a formality. Even being around her Sunday school students was a struggle because she saw the joy having children can bring while not being able to experience it, and she yearned for her babies more in the way that you yearn for something you never had. It seemed like everyone else around her age already had one, two, or three children of their own! She was depressed. This was a rock-bottom hit, and it seemed like she sank lower into the pits of depression by the day. No matter how much her husband, friends, and family tried, she wouldn't be lifted out.

After the second miscarriage, they tried to conceive again, to no avail. They went for various tests and checkups, and all of them came back with results showing that they were okay. There were lots of *do*s and *don't*s from some apparently super-fertile people like staying off soft cheese, red wine, rare steak, and smoked salmon. She became obsessed with pregnancy tests. The double line on the pregnancy test kit never appeared, and she drifted further from her friends as they embarked on new phases of their lives that she couldn't follow.

She and Johnny gradually drifted apart. She could sense the walls going up between them, but she lacked the strength to do anything about it. Even lovemaking became like work; pleasure and enjoyment went out of it. Eventually, Johnny started staying away from home longer than usual under the guise of work. Their home became void of laughter and peace. He became irritated with her mood swings while she saw him as unaffectionate and uncaring; she was bitter.

In their sixth year of marriage, they were referred to a specialist, and upon thorough examination, she was diagnosed with a medical condition that made it difficult to get pregnant because the cysts blocked her fallopian tubes. The good news was that they could be removed with surgery. Hope that had wilted sprang up to life like a dead tree at the scent of water. She desperately wished that this would be the breakthrough she'd been looking for.

She became friends with God again, and that hope gave her something to live for again. The surgery was successful, and things were fine for a year. There was no sign of pregnancy, but there was hope. Close to their eighth wedding anniversary, she started feeling some mild pain in her pelvis. The pain became worse by the day, and it was accompanied by a bloated feeling. On one faithful afternoon, she attempted to rise from the dining room table where she sat, but the pain was so much that she fainted. She woke up some hours later to learn that she had a ruptured ovary, for which she bled for three days where it was located. She had surgery that led to more surgeries because some new cysts formed and caused uncontrollable pain.

As if things couldn't get any worse, she stopped menstruating, and nothing worked for her, not even her hormones. Eleven years into her marriage, she was told by her doctor that she would be unable to have a child of her own. At this point, her life was the upside down of upside down. Adoption remained the only option.

A year later, they started the adoption process, and for some unknown reason, it did not work out. They gave up after the second attempt and were resigned to fate. Early in the following year, she slept one day and had the most unusual dream. She lay on a beach while a little boy was playing in the shallow parts of the water. She was keeping half an eye on him. He bent down to pick coral shells, came out of the water, and laid them at her feet, giggling.

The dream only brought back the yearnings of her yesteryears, the things that could have been, should have been, the pain, the frustration, the anger. She wept repeatedly like a baby while the wounds she thought had healed became fresh again. She lay there in the presence of her Savior: broken, weak, helpless, defeated, and pained. How could her one attempt at life be so miserable? There she lay with her first love and fell into a deep peaceful sleep. Jesus spoke and said, "*Get up! Come with Me, and you'll be delivered. I'll show you how to truly rest.*"

From that point onwards, the focus of her life was changed, and there was a peace and calmness around her that was so real it could almost be touched. She made peace with God, her husband, her family, her friends, and her acquaintances. No longer was she going to be choked by her quest for a child. She was going to wait on God and trust in Him.

On a fateful summer day, she discovered that she had some light bleeding and went to her doctor for an examination. After examinations and cross-examinations, employing all the expertise of the medical profession, it was discovered that she was two months pregnant. She still could not believe the report. It took further examinations from another hospital to convince her. This was real, and it was happening!

She dropped to her knees right there in the hospital room and began to give God glory. She praised Him with tears of joy in her eyes. God did not forget about her. She stood up and realized her family was not there to rejoice with her. She immediately grabbed her phone out of her pocket and began to dial her husband. She screamed, "I'm pregnant! We're pregnant! We're having a baby!"

Johnny could barely understand what she was saying because she was screaming, crying, and laughing all at the same time. Johnny asked her to calm down and repeat herself. She could not contain herself. She said it again, and she heard Johnny scream on the other end, "I'm having a baby!" She could hear his coworkers in the background congratulating him. They both smiled from ear to ear. They promised to wait another two months before telling anyone else their amazing news. They wanted to get the clearance after the first trimester was over, which is when most of the risks are over. But unfortunately for her, her entire pregnancy term would be a risk.

It was the most difficult time for her, holding her secret in and not sharing the wonderful news with her loved ones. Two months later, she made her rounds of calling her parents, the rest of her family, and her girlfriends. Everyone was elated for her, but she could hear it in their tone of voice that some were weary and doubted a successful pregnancy. They warned her not to get too excited because of her previous experiences. But Hope did not care about that! She believed in this miracle that God allowed her after doctors told her she would not be able to have any children. She trusted God and had faith that He would bring her through this. She could not wait to meet her little one.

She was extra careful about everything—what she ate, how she moved, how she laid, everything. Johnny tended to her every need and made sure she was comfortable. He attended every doctor's checkup appointment with her. They prayed every night together that God would have His way with them and would bless them with a healthy baby.

God showed His miraculous ways six months later with the birth of little Carter! Xoxo!

Scripture Reflections

1. Trust in God, for He is the one Who will bring you out. In Psalm 62:5–7,

    Yes, my soul, find rest in God; my hope comes from him. Truly he is my rock and my salvation; he is my fortress; I will not be shaken. My salvation and my honor depend on God; he is my mighty rock, my refuge.

2. Even the winds and the waves obey God! God turns a hopeless situation around in a blink of an eye. In Matthew 8:26,

    The Lord replied, "You of little faith, why are you so afraid?" Then he got up and rebuked the winds and the waves, and it was completely calm.

3. God doesn't lie and keeps His promises to us. In Hebrews 10:23,

    Let us hold unswervingly to the hope we profess, for he who promised is faithful.

4. In Jeremiah 29:11–14,

    For I know the plans I have for you, declares the Lord, plans to prosper you and not to harm you, plans to give you hope and a future. Then you will call on me, and I will listen to you. You will seek me and find me when you seek me with all your heart. I will be found by you, declares the Lord, and will bring you back from captivity.

5. In Psalm 33:18–19,

 But the eyes of the Lord are on those whose hope is in his unfailing love, to deliver them from death and keep them alive in famine.

6. In Isaiah 40:31,

 But those who hope in the Lord will renew their strength. They will soar on wings like eagles; they will run and not grow weary; they will walk and not be faint.

7. In Romans 8:24–28,

 We were given this hope when we were saved. (If we already have something, we don't need to hope for it. But if we look forward to something we don't yet have, we must wait patiently and confidently.) And the Holy Spirit helps us in our weakness. For example, we don't know what God wants us to pray for. But the Holy Spirit prays for us with groanings that cannot be expressed in words. And the Father who knows all hearts knows what the Spirit is saying, for the Spirit pleads for us believers in harmony with God's own will. And we know that God causes everything to work together for the good of those who love God and are called according to his purpose for them.

Let Us Pray

Dear Lord, Savior of the world, hear my cry. Just like Hope in her story, I need You. Your Word says, Lord, that You will never leave me nor forsake me. Establish my hope in You. I believe in You. May Your Word strengthen my soul and may the purpose of God in my life be fulfilled that through endurance and through the encouragement of the scriptures, You might give me hope. I pray for determination in my heart to always choose to hope continually and praise You more and more no matter the situation I am in. I pray that I may be of encouragement to others when their hope is fading. May the eyes of my understanding be enlightening to know the hope of my calling in Christ Jesus. Thank You for Your grace and Your mercy. In Jesus Christ's name, I pray, amen!

Notes

II

Joy

Bloody discomposure on his face, a cut upper lip, scuffed shoes, and a bloodstained shirt—he made quite a pretty picture. The secretary couldn't help but stare at him and mutter something about irresponsible parenting, to which he responded with a defiant stare of his own. Why wouldn't the old lady let him be? She kept throwing him sorry looks from behind the telephone, and the last thing he needed now was a pity party.

He heard his father's secretary say over the phone that he was incredibly busy and had given stern instructions not to be disturbed even when she was told that it was about his son and quite urgent. His mother was out of town at a conference. How splendid that everyone was always busy, and no one treated him as if he had even the tiniest importance.

He didn't care though, or so that's what he told himself. The secretary turned to him muttering something about not being able to reach any of his parents, and when she asked him for any other means of contacting them, he pretended not to hear her and inwardly started counting the dots on the polka-dotted curtain. He was obviously trying to be tough, but that didn't quite take away his angelic looks. He had to make a trip to the school clinic where the nurse wiped some mud off his skin, cleaned his cuts with antiseptic, and gave him a drink of water. He lay for a while on a nearby bed and thought about stuff. When the nurse saw that he was getting restless, she shooed him back to the reception where he feigned sleep but was actually thinking of the fight that got him in the mess he was in.

That crazy Brett was trying to bully Spencer, who was sort of the smallest boy in their class. That afternoon, they were pushing him around and shoving him against the lockers while the poor boy shivered and muttered something inaudibly. He'd told the bully to let him be, but Brett only laughed in his face and told him it was not his business, and then he saw red. The next thing he knew, Brett was on the floor holding his bloodied nose, with blood on his shirt and hands, and the rest of the pack had scattered.

It was quite unfortunate that the principal saw him in this state and immediately jumped to conclusions. Brett was a master actor and told such an incredible lie that no sane adult should believe him, but he successfully labeled himself as the victim, which meant that he was in deep trouble. He doubted if there was going to be another chance for him, not that he wanted one.

The ringing of the telephone jarred him from his thoughts and brought him back to the present. Apparently, his mother had been contacted after what seemed like an eternity and was on her way back to pick him up.

After waiting for a few hours, his mom showed up, looking like she just stepped out of some fashion magazine. Boy, she sure knew how to dress. Despite his present predicament, he was happy to see her, but the same couldn't be said for his mom since her only acknowledgment of his presence was a scathing glance that could make even the devil pee his pants. He winced inwardly, and his mouth fell.

Joy was devastated. She didn't know what to do with her twelve-year-old son. He was always getting into fights and beating up some kids in school. His anger issues were getting worse by the day, and it seemed like he only existed to lash out at the world. This was the third school her son Michael attended in two years, and he was getting the ax again. It took every fiber in her to restrain her from crying in the principal's office. She couldn't quite figure out why her son was hell-bent on throwing away his chances at a good education. Even before he got into the fight with Brett, he had received countless warnings since midsemester on how he wasn't taking his studies seriously. He was failing most of the subjects, but he couldn't care less, so it didn't matter that it was four days until vacation or that he got into a fight; they were going to kick him out anyways.

His mother spent quite a long time in the principal's office, so he tried guessing what he was saying to his mother. He thought to himself that the principal was probably going on and on about his consistency with breaking rules, how he was a bad influence, and how sorry his grades were while his mother would most likely plead earnestly with a pained expression for him not to be kicked out because she was busy, and no school would probably accept him.

For an instant, he felt kind of sorry that he put her in such a position, but if it was about beating Brett, he'd probably do it a million times over even if it meant he wasn't going to be accepted in any other school. On a more serious note, if he continued this way, he was probably going to end up being illiterate. That thought cracked him up. The receptionist gave him a look that said she was irritated with his loud laughter, but he couldn't care less. So he went outside and contented himself kicking up the grass while humming a tune.

After some time, his mother came out of the principal's office and started toward him with a furious look in her eyes. He sure made a mess of things this time. His bags were packed into the car's trunk, and they headed home. For the first half of the journey, he pretended to be asleep so as not to further incur his mother's wrath, and then he leaned his head against the window and watched the passing scenery—the hills, the vegetation, and the landscapes—while he pretended not to listen to her yell at his father over the phone. Obviously, he was the subject of their argument.

His mom was looking for a way to push him off to his father's house, but his father was not having it. He had a vacation planned with his new girlfriend, and the idea of a third party was distasteful. His mom cut the call with a well-aimed barbed remark with a cloying sweet tone. From the look of things, it seemed he was stuck with his mom since she couldn't push him off to his dad's. He was depressed.

What is it about me that always makes people not want me? he wondered. His mom never seemed to want him around, and his dad barely acknowledged his existence. They were parents who were always pushing him off; even schools did the same. The tears fell even though he promised himself that he wasn't going to care or shed a single tear again. He would give his right arm for the tiniest bit of love or affection. When he could no longer bear the thick silence, he turned on the radio in the car, but his mom would have none of it, so she turned it off and still didn't say anything about the incident that led to his recent expulsion. After staring in silence for so long, he drifted off to sleep, and the next thing he knew, they were home.

It was midnight, and Joy couldn't sleep. Whichever way she looked at it, she was unable to wrap her finger around how she got her life into such a mess. Her husband walked out of her life, and she still had not gotten over the pain from their shattered relationship. It hurt to be used and discarded. Her son was another matter entirely. Why was Michael doing this to her? Why was he so rebellious and angry at everyone? She had provided him with everything he needed, or at least she showed that she loved him by giving him everything he wanted. She especially made sure that he got the best of everything, including those things she couldn't dream of having as a kid. It wasn't her fault that his father can be vile sometimes. Why couldn't he remain the sweet little boy he used to be when he was little? Joy asked herself all these questions.

As a family counselor, Joy had helped many families to resolve their marital issues. She helped parents who were estranged from their teenagers to reach out to them. She really understood those teenagers and had worked with many to overcome substance abuse, addiction, and peer pressure, and their parents were always grateful. She was quite good at what she did since advising people came naturally to her. She was a go-getter and had worked to build the practice she now had. She was a very busy person as she had to attend workshops, seminars, and conferences across the world to stay relevant in her game. She received her bachelor's degree in social work, master's degree in marriage and family counseling, and doctorate degree in counseling psychology. She wasn't from an affluent background, so she had to push through college on student loans and scholarships. She was the first of four daughters who her tough mom had raised single-handedly on a secretary's income.

Growing up wasn't much of a palatable experience. She knew what it meant to not have, and that was why she made sure that her son never lacked anything. She envied other girls her age. To her, it wasn't fair that all the other girls had plenty of pretty things while she had none at all and that they had plenty of time for leisure and frivolities while she had to babysit and work to assist her mother and her sisters.

It was dreadful to be poor, but that was not to say that she wasn't grateful for how hard her mom worked to give them at least a decent life. She loved her mom even though they had many differences. Her little sisters were darlings, and she was a mother figure to them since their mom had to work most of the time and wasn't around. They always took their problems to her and confided in her all their little don't-tell-moms. She, on the other hand, was compassionate and kind and always gave them a listening ear. She had a gift of understanding people from quite an early age.

Despite their poverty, Joy had many friends and was popular. Her personality attracted people, and her good nature combined with her smart brain and beautiful physique made her a wonderful package. Her mom sure had high expectations for her.

Growing up, she was grateful to have her clique, which consisted of her three other friends. They were more than enough compensation for the material things she lacked. When she was with them, she couldn't be bothered about her old dresses or worn-out shoes. In the clique, Joy was their unofficial counselor. They related all their boy problems, family drama, and academic problems to her because she always listened and understood them somehow and gave sensible advice. She even helped them to get out of trouble with their parents and some arguments they got themselves in. She was really a girl's best friend. Watching out for others came naturally to her, and she was staunchly loyal.

Even when they became young women, she was somehow good at predicting guys. She could predict if the relationship wasn't going to last, and most of her predictions were often true, so she ended up giving plenty of relationship advice to her friends.

She decided to become a counselor in her sophomore year of high school after she spent her summer days interning in a social services office. She realized she could put her passion and talent for helping people out with their problems to good use even though her momma thought that it was a waste of her smart brain.

She met Alex in her first year of college at a conference thrown for freshmen students. She thought he was the most handsome man she had ever seen, and when they got talking, she couldn't blame herself for falling in love with him. He was on fire for the Lord and full of ambitions and good ideas for his ministry. He was every woman's dream. He not only looked good, but he was also good, and she counted herself fortunate to have him.

They kept in touch and spent most of their vacations together on one mission or another. They got engaged after a year of dating, and she took him home to her momma. She could tell that momma didn't approve of him, and she couldn't think of any reasons since she thought her Alex was perfect.

They got married immediately after graduation, and she was a loving and caring wife, eager to please. She completely idolized her husband. He became an associate pastor at his father's friend's church, which provided them with accommodation. She gave him the full support he needed in his ministry, and while he was very busy in those days, she started her master's program since there was no child to look after yet. Eventually, Alex was transferred to a church in the big city while she took up work at a nearby university. Somehow, she managed to balance her career with supporting her husband in his ministry. She became their church counselor. Those were hard and trying times, but they endured and loved each other.

Michael was born in the third year of their marriage, and their marriage seemed like the most perfect one. They were one happy family, time passed, and her husband's ministry flourished, so she had to give up her work at the university. The church members loved her kind nature, her gentle spirit, and her compassion. She was always settling one family issue or another. Her husband's ministry took him on many travels; he was a constantly busy person and didn't have time to spare for his son.

Trouble started with their son misbehaving at school. Her husband was always being impatient with him. She also got to discover the true nature of her husband. He was never physically abusive but threw words that came in like grenades. He grew irritated at the slightest things she did and could barely stand her presence.

While things deteriorated at home, she tried to maintain the appearance of a successful marriage while she prayed, fasted, and did a whole lot of things to win her husband back. She was ever the counselor, helping many families bridge their gaps while the chasm separating her own family grew wider still. She got to find out that her husband was cheating on her with other women during his travels. There was no one she could talk to about her situation and her marriage. She kept up the smile and the charade of things being perfect. She quickly discovered that the whole marriage was a joke. She couldn't continue putting up the "all is well" façade, and to avoid causing a major uproar, she took her son and left. Oh, how she hurt.

She moved to another state to start a new life entirely. She enrolled Michael in one of the best private schools and worked from home as a marriage therapist. He was the striking figure of his father and reminded her of him every time. She became angry, frustrated, and bitter. She poured herself into her work as a therapist, deliberately made herself busy, and traveled so much that she barely spent time with Michael.

Michael was forced to learn to do things on his own and fend for himself at an early age since he didn't like to ask the babysitter for any help or anything for that matter. He lacked love and affection, but Joy had none for him, and this heightened Michael's anger toward her and life. Joy had no love in her to give as she felt it was all taken away by her ungrateful husband. She did quite fine for herself and set up her own private practice which flourished.

Life had gone on. She learned to bury her hurt and mask her pains well. She still helped families with their problems in her own practical and professional way. The part of her that tried to point people in the way of God was gone, though. She felt empty most of the time. Her son was the only big issue; she was confused about what to do with him.

She went to his room and stood over his bed, watching his angelic features. She remembered the love and excitement she felt when she first held him in her arms, the feeling of tenderness, and how he had been the sunshine in her life. The angry scowl he wore was off his face now, and he looked like her baby once more. She saw a child fighting desperately for the love she was incapable of giving—a child hurt and seeking attention through whatever means.

In her hurt and frustration, she had pushed him away, thus betraying him and leaving him in the lurch. She made a mess of her life and was doing the same for her son. She really felt his pain of not having a father's love and losing the friend he has in his mother because she was buried deep in her own pain. She ached for her son. She had let her bitterness consume her, and now even her baby was suffering for it.

She needed help, and she knew it. Her momma would be ready with all her strength to say, "I told you so." She had not been to church in a long time, and she couldn't even remember the last time she prayed. She had turned away from God's outstretched hands and refused His healing and comfort. She had given the enemy room to play her like a deck of cards.

Gazing at her son's face, she wept and fell to her knees. She began to pray for herself, her husband, her son, and every marriage going through tough times. She realized that she had put everything else first in front of God. She wanted to rebuild her relationship with God, so she simply talked to Him. She started to make time to talk to God in the morning, at noon, and at night. All those things she wanted to share with the world, she just shared them with God despite her knowing that God already knew everything going on. She depended on God to hear her stories every day.

After weeks of meditation and conversations with God, she began to include Michael in her prayer time. At first, Michael was hesitant to join his mother, but he then started to see this time with his mother as a precious time when he was receiving the love and affection he always longed for. While he didn't know exactly how to pray, he just listened every time as his mother prayed and coached him to say *amen* at the end.

More weeks and months went by, and Michael finally found the courage to ask his mother to let him pray this time. Stunned by the request, Joy just smiled and waited for his debut. She was so proud of her baby boy. He prayed for their family and for love and peace. The innocence and sincerity in him brought Joy to tears. While she didn't restore her relationship with her husband, she did regain her relationship with God and her son, which she missed so dearly.

At the end of his prayer, Joy held Michael tight in her arms and just wept. She promised to love and cherish him the way a mother was supposed to. She promised to be there for him always. Michael took it all in as he wept along with her.

Scripture Reflections

1. We go through the trials and tribulations of life with God by our side. In Psalm 30:1–5,

    I will exalt you, Lord, for you lifted me out of the depths and did not let my enemies gloat over me. Lord my God, I called to you for help, and you healed me. You, Lord, brought me up from the realm of the dead; you spared me from going down to the pit. Sing the praises of the Lord, you his faithful people; praise his holy name. For his anger lasts only a moment, but his favor lasts a lifetime; weeping may stay for the night, but rejoicing comes in the morning.

2. Regardless of what you do, He will always love you. In Isaiah 62:5,

    As a young man marries a young woman, so will your Builder marry you; as a bridegroom rejoices over his bride, so will your God rejoice over you.

3. In Romans 15:13,

    May the God of hope fill you with all joy and peace as you trust in him, so that you may overflow with hope by the power of the Holy Spirit.

4. Know who you are! You are a child of God! In Proverbs 23:22–25,

    Listen to your father, who gave you life, and do not despise your mother when she is old. Buy the truth and do not sell it—wisdom, instruction and insight as well. The father of a righteous child has

great joy; a man who fathers a wise son rejoices in him. May your father and mother rejoice; may she who gave you birth be joyful!

5. Your pain is temporary. Ask the Lord for your joy, and He will bring you through. In John 16:21–24,

    A woman giving birth to a child has pain because her time has come; but when her baby is born she forget the anguish because of her joy that a child is born into the world. So with you: Now is your time of grief, but I will see you again and you will rejoice, and no one will take away your joy. In that day you will no longer ask anything, very truly I tell you, my Father will give you whatever you ask in my name. Until now you have not asked for anything in my name. Ask and you will receive, and your joy will be complete.

6. In 2 Corinthians 13:5–11,

    Examine yourselves to see whether you are in the faith; test yourselves. Do you not realize that Christ Jesus is in you—unless, of course, you fail the test? And I trust that you will discover that we have not failed the test. Now we pray to God that you will not do anything wrong—not so that people will see that we have stood the test but so that you will do what is right even though we may seem to have failed. For we cannot do anything against the truth, but only for the truth. We are glad whenever we are weak but you are strong; and our prayer is that you may be fully restored. This is why I write these things when I am absent, that when I come I may not have to be harsh in my use of authority— the authority the Lord gave me for building you up, not for tearing you down. Finally, brothers and sisters, rejoice! Strive for full restoration, encourage one another, be of one mind, live in peace. And the God of love and peace will be with you.

7. Put God first, and He will see that you find joy in the end. In Isaiah 58:13–14,

> *If you keep your feet from breaking the Sabbath and from doing as you please on my holy day, if you call the Sabbath a delight and the Lord's holy day honorable, and if you honor it by not going your own way and not doing as you please or speaking idle words, then you will find your joy in the Lord, and I will cause you to ride in triumph on the heights of the land and to feast on the inheritance of your father Jacob. The mouth of the Lord has spoken.*

Let Us Pray

Dear Lord, Savior of the world, hear my cry. Just like Joy in her story, please forgive me. I have not always put You first. Instead, I consumed myself with work and money, other people, and other things. Your first commandment tells us, Lord, to not have any other God but You. Help me to put everything else behind You and seek You first. You are Lord of my life, and I will praise Your name forever. Restore the joy of my salvation. I acknowledge that without You, I am nothing, I have nothing, and I can do nothing. Have Your way in my life as I seek You first in all that I do. Uproot any bad seeds I have sown. Destroy the negative things in my life. I choose You, Lord. Help me to love again just as You love us. Thank You for Your grace and Your mercy. In Jesus Christ's name, I pray, amen!

Notes

III

Faith

It was 3:00 a.m., and the phone vibrated, disturbing my sleep. I wondered who could be calling or texting at that time of the night. I tossed and turned in bed, blocking off the vibration with my pillow, and it stopped to my relief. I had a long, stressful day, and my batteries weren't well recharged yet. A few minutes after, it started vibrating again, and I cursed inwardly as I forced myself out of bed toward it. No sooner had I gotten to it, and then it stopped again. I was so tired that I didn't even bother to check the caller ID to see the missed calls.

I headed back to bed again, and I was just settling in when it started vibrating again, this time for a longer time. At this point, I was livid, and I flew out of bed determined to just turn the phone off, and I would have if I hadn't noticed that it was my friend Faith.

Muffled sobs and sniffles greet me on the other end. I said *hello*, but there was no response, only more sobs and a long pause. I said *hello* again, and this time, she said, "It's me." The first thing that ran through my mind was that someone died or that one of the kids got hurt. I remembered that she'd called me the previous week, but I was too busy to return any of her calls. She was trying to say something I couldn't decipher, and I heard running water and assumed she was in the bathroom. After several minutes, I succeeded in calming her down and getting out of her what the problem was. I promised her that I was going to head over to her place first thing the next morning and hung up, but not before I extracted from her a promise not to do anything crazy before I came. Thankfully, it was the start of my two-week vacation even though it was a lousy way of starting a vacation I have so much wanted for a needed rest.

All the thought of sleep had departed and was replaced by that of my dear Faith unable to sleep, crying out her eyes in her bathroom at 3:00 a.m. I tried forcing the disturbing picture out of my head and cajoled myself to sleep. My mind won after all, so I got out of bed, wrapped myself in a robe, and went into my kitchen where I fixed myself a tea and let my thoughts wander.

Faith and I were best friends even before we walked or even said our first words. We grew up together in the same neighborhood. Our mothers claim that our first words were each other's names. I don't quite believe it, but I think there might be some elements of truth in that. Our mothers were best friends, the same as our fathers, so we were practically stuck with each other. We grew up having playdates at the nearby school playground, playing house, planning on running away together, and always going over to each other's homes.

I remember one incident when we were three, my mother was doing some sewing and carelessly left her sewing basket which had a pair of scissors close by. Before she came, we had a most delightful time taking turns snipping off each other's hair. I'll never forget the look of horror on my mother's face as she came in time to stop us from snipping off each other's ears. But much damage was already done; the rest of our hair had to be cut off. We went to school together and were in the same class each year. I was the outspoken and mischievous one, always getting into arguments; she was the pretty one, rather reserved and shy, the model child of our busy neighborhood. Many of my earliest memories were of her, memories that still bring a smile to my face.

We stuck together through elementary and middle school before that troublemaker Lawrence intruded into our lives and our friendship. Lawrence was the new neighbor's son who moved next door to my house when we were in the seventh grade. He was about our age and was always in a lot of trouble. On his very first day in our school, he wound up Ms. Brown until she was as tight as a clock, and her nerves were on end. Then he got into a fight with Gerald, our class bully who was twice his size and height, during lunch period. It took all the influence and persuasion of his father not to get him kicked out of school after spending just a few hours there.

At first, he hung out with a bunch of troublemakers like himself before he would get kicked out of their midst for God knows what. He was quite happy causing trouble alone before he got bored and lonely because parents had warned their kids not to associate with him. No right-thinking girl would talk to him after he put a bug in another girl's hair and brought crickets to class and let them loose in math class. But that didn't take away his divine looks. How could he still look like an angel after all those atrocities listed?

I noticed he always liked to play tag with Faith and me. Faith was so scared of him. I warned him off several times, but he would just laugh and continue his annoying ways. He was a terrible pest; he was always interrupting our lunches and activities. When we finally asked him what he wanted, he said he didn't mind being the third wheel in our friendship. No way! We much rather invite the devil to be our buddy than allow him into our circle. There was no escaping from him. He hounded us for a long time until we granted him membership into our friendship on our terms. We made him sign an agreement to comply with all our rules and run odd errands for us whenever we so wished and kick him out if he ever caused any trouble. Somehow funny anyways, but he stayed.

Little did we expect that he was going to behave like an angel and in every way become a loyal friend. We didn't let our guard down and always examined his intent with suspicion. I liked him a lot because we were alike in many ways: wild, adventurous, impulsive, mischievous, witty, and always coming up with crazy stuff to do spontaneously. Faith liked him too and soon got used to his rascal ways. We got to discover that beneath all the troublemaking, he was a good person and soft inside as opposed to the hard, tough image he projected. In fact, he was a huge fan of Mickey Mouse, so we fondly nicknamed him Toodles. He was always running errands for us. I was quite a hard taskmaster and contributed a lot to our fun ideas. We fought frequently because we both had a short fuse while Faith was always the peacemaker.

Things changed a lot the summer of our eighth grade when I went on vacation with my family and came back to discover a disturbing closeness between Lawrence and Faith. I tried asking them what was up, but Faith would just blush beet red while the other one would tease me with a smug look on his face and an annoying whistle. I felt it was because I was away and that things would normalize, but that didn't happen.

I started feeling left out of whatever secret they had and grew more anxious by the day. It finally dawned on me one day that Lawrence had stolen my best friend from me. I always knew that boy was no good! I saw the way he looked at her. I went home in tears. That was too big a betrayal for me. I was shattered. I didn't blame Faith much because I was quite sure that the rogue did something to her. I had always known that boy had been no good from the start. How could I not have known that he was a friend thief? I started wishing for him to disappear one day so that I could have my best friend back though I sort of felt guilty; he was also my friend.

They started dating officially in our freshmen year of high school; even in middle school, everyone knew they were sweethearts. It was not an uncommon sight to see him spinning my friend around in the hallway while whistling or kissing her before math class, to my utmost disgust. She failed math that year. That boy was bad luck, and her father had to restrict her from seeing him. His own grades were far worse, but then again, when did Lawrence ever care about his grades?

The restriction didn't last for long since Lawrence surely knew how to work his way around rules. Sweet, loving, helpful Faith worked magic on him where his parents and teachers tried but failed severely. She got him to apply himself to his studies; she practically became his tutor, and his grades improved tremendously to the amazement of his parents. She made him work hard, but he never quite became an A student. He had hopes of going to college.

In our senior year, they were voted the best couple. They would have gotten married straight out of high school, but Faith's dad wouldn't have it. Trouble came when they got accepted into separate universities far from each other. I thought that would be the end of their relationship, for young love doesn't last long. To my surprise, they got together at every opportunity that school breaks afforded them. They stuck together and pushed it through despite all odds.

After graduating from college, Lawrence and Faith landed jobs in separate cities, forcing them to have a long-distance relationship. They flew back and forth every six weeks to see each other. After two years, they were finally able to relocate to the same city where they've lived together since then and were in no rush to get married any longer. They wanted to work for a while and pay off the debts they acquired as students. But things don't always go as planned. Faith got pregnant after a year of living together and gave birth the following year to a baby boy. Lawrence proposed at the birth of their first child, and so they started their family together. She got pregnant again three years later and gave birth to a set of twins. When the twins were a year old, they got married and moved to the suburbs.

True to my word, I packed my bags and left my home in the city at the first light of dawn and headed toward her home. It was a nice three-hour drive door-to-door. As I pulled into the driveway, I saw Faith opening the front door. I ran to put my arms around her, hugging her close. "My love," she said and started crying. "I'm glad you came." When I arrived, the children had already left for school.

Not quite sure of what to say, I held her close for a while, caressing her hair while she cried to her heart's content. She grew quiet after a while and apologized. I told her it was okay and that I knew how to swim, so tears couldn't drown me, and we both laughed. I had noticed the dark circles under her eyes. She always looked like that when she was in trouble. I could bet she wasn't sleeping or eating well. My heart ached for my best friend. We stood there, embracing each other for about five minutes before I really went in. I had missed her terribly.

"What time do the children get back from school?" I asked.

"Around six," she answered. She let go of me slowly.

"We'll have plenty of time to talk before they get back."

"How about a glass of wine?" she asked.

"That would be fine."

Faith took two glasses from the cupboard and a bottle of wine from the fridge, and we moved into the living room. "Where is your stuff?"

"I left them in the car. I'll bring them in later."

I studied her closely. She had lost weight and looked like the shadow of her old self. We sat down there in uncomfortable silence for a few minutes, sipping wine, while my eyes studied my surroundings. "You have quite a nice home here," I said, breaking the silence. She thanked me and was silent again. I was going to say something else when she cleared her throat and asked me where she should start narrating her story. I told her I wanted to hear the whole story.

She started by telling me how barely two years into their new home, she noticed that her husband was staying away from home longer than usual and would give ridiculous accounts of where he was, what he was doing, or who the people he was with. She knew that his stories weren't adding up, and when she brought it to his attention, he became defensive and said she was accusing him. Gradually, he grew distant from her and found ways of being excused from things they did together. He wasn't as caring and loving as he used to be, and she noticed how he stopped making conversation with her. Always the peacemaker, she apologized countless times for whatever she did that was making him act up. He grew irritated with her and snapped at her even at the slightest mistakes. And how he would turn down all her attempts at lovemaking.

Things came to a head when she noticed that he moved his stuff into the guest bedroom. The children could also feel the tension between their parents and the little things they used to love, and affection grew miserable. She was blind, deaf, foolish, and couldn't read him or perhaps ignored the writing on the wall. She prayed and prayed, but the situation of things still did not change. Instead, her husband spent longer time away from home.

One day, she answered his phone while he was in the bathroom, and the person at the other end didn't realize that it was his wife who picked up the phone. He walked in at that instant, and he knew she was deeply hurt at his betrayal, but he didn't seem to care. Then he came home one day and presented divorce papers, saying that he was tired of the marriage. She refused even with the immense pressure mounted on her. He packed his things from home gradually. The day before she called me, he left and said he wasn't coming back.

By the time she was done with her story, I was in tears with her. I promised myself that I was going to beat him to a pulp the moment I set my eyes on him. How could anyone want to hurt a woman like Faith, who was faithful, loyal, and loving? My head started hurting. What was worse is that I knew the jerk from childhood; we were even friends. I wondered how people change suddenly. She told the children that their dad was traveling when in reality he was going to be with another woman. The first love that once warmed the house was gone. My God!

The tiredness that had begun in me after her narration remained over me. As I watched the petals and twigs that swayed outside the window, there was only a creeping sorrow where there once was a joy. It seemed to have sat like a November rain on my skin, enough to chill what was once warm inside. Any other time, my friend would call me and ask for the warmth she needed to make a situation better.

The sound of kids arriving made us compose ourselves as we didn't want them to suspect anything. My anger was forgotten for a moment as her kids flung themselves at me. I completely adored them. We went out to get my stuff from the car and were more than delighted to see the goodies I bought for them at a mall I stopped by on my way. I was sad again wondering how someone leaves such a beautiful family behind. It was really his loss. I was jarred out of my thoughts by her daughter. She thought my bracelets were cool, so I slipped one off my hand onto hers and was rewarded with a dazzling smile that warmed my heart.

We started making plans on how to get her back on her feet as she quit her job after she had the twins. She had always wanted to start her own business, so we brainstormed freelancing ideas where she could help others and be creative by planning events.

She was depressed, so we researched group and individual therapy sessions for women going through similar situations like her. We managed to schedule some recurring appointments for her to attend in the next several weeks. We prayed every night I was there, and I encouraged her to continue to pray with me every night on the phone. I stayed for a week, after which I had to go back home. The children were sad to see me go and made me promise to come back soon.

We kept in touch frequently, speaking and praying every night, and she updated me on how things were going. We prayed for forgiveness, for the Lord to comfort her heart as she was still grieving the separation from her husband, and for a financial breakthrough. Six months later, she landed a job earning decent pay, enough to maintain her monthly bills that weren't being held up by her husband since he was too busy playing house with someone else.

I tried contacting Lawrence to no avail. He wouldn't return any of my calls or text messages. As luck would have it, almost two years later, I ran into him in the city. He looked quite shocked to see me. He looked as if life itself had grabbed him, chewed him up, and spit him back out. He was a lot skinnier than I could remember. You could tell that life was not treating him good at all. I know I said that I would punch him in the face when I saw him, and my mind surely went there, but the only thing that my mouth could utter was, "I've been praying for you." I walked away feeling sorry for him. I couldn't even tell Faith that I saw him because I didn't want to open her wound again. Instead, I just continued to pray for him with Faith.

Despite his absence from the house for so long, Faith still yearned for his return one day. She was willing to forgive and forget all that he has done and move on. She wanted so badly to just move forward and be a happy family again. But it seemed like the more she prayed for that, the more time he spent out partying, living the single life, and not worrying about her.

It wasn't until her prayers changed that her life changed. We began to pray for a change in her heart, a transformation in her mind, forgiveness, love, and healing. We prayed that she would accept the things that were coming her way and that the Lord would help her get through them, whatever they may be. We prayed that the Lord has His will and His way with Faith and her family. We left it in the Lord's hands now. She focused on herself and her children. She started to incorporate her children into the prayers. She began to do things for herself and with others. She was no longer depressed sitting at home thinking of her ex-husband.

She heard wind from a mutual friend that her ex-husband was not looking too good and how he managed to let himself go. She couldn't afford to take her emotions back to where they were when she longed for him and nothing more. However, she was saddened by the news. She continued to pray long and hard for him. She closed her eyes and envisioned herself being held by him again. She opened her eyes and shrugged the vision off as tears flowed down her cheeks. She couldn't forget the hurt and pain he put her through. She has forgiven him but loved herself more now to go back to that. Faith wiped her tears, whispered a prayer, and strut along in her heels to work.

Scripture Reflections

1. In 2 Corinthians 5:7,

    For we live by faith, not by sight.

2. God knows your pains, the things you have lost in your life, your lost relationships, dreams, past mistakes, lost investments, failed issues, and projects. However, God can restore you in abundance. In Isaiah 61:7,

    Instead of your shame you will receive a double portion, and instead of disgrace you will rejoice in your inheritance. And so you will inherit a double portion in your land, and everlasting joy will be yours.

3. Our God is a restorer. He is ready to restore all your wasted years and put an end to all chronic delays. God knows your need. He will compensate you for time lost, and He will wipe away your years of sorrow, toiling, and waiting. In Job 42:10–12,

    After Job had prayed for his friends, the Lord restored his fortunes and gave him twice as much as he had before. All his brothers and sisters and everyone who had known him before came and ate with him in his house. They comforted and consoled him over all the trouble the Lord had brought on him, each one gave him a piece of silver and a gold ring. The Lord blessed the latter part of Job's life more than the former part.

4. Despite your current situation, God knows all about it and will make sure to bring you through. In Job 8:7,

   Your beginnings will seem humble, so prosperous will your future be.

5. Those times and situations in your life that you believe have been ruined and destroyed, God can transform them into something beautiful and glorious. You may not see it now, but tomorrow will come, and you will see the beauty in His works. In Isaiah 61:1–3,

   The Spirit of the Sovereign Lord is on me, because the Lord has anointed me to proclaim good news to the poor. He has sent me to bind up the brokenhearted, to proclaim freedom for the captives and release from darkness for the prisoners, to proclaim the year of the Lord's favor and the day of vengeance of our God, to comfort all who mourn, and provide for those who grieve in Zion—to bestow on them a crown of beauty instead of ashes, the oil of joy instead of mourning, and a garment of praise instead of a spirit of despair. They will be called oaks of righteousness, a planting of the Lord for the display of his splendor.

6. In Matthew 6:33–34,

   But seek first his kingdom and his righteousness, and all these things will be given to you as well. Therefore, do not worry about tomorrow, for tomorrow will worry about itself. Each day has enough trouble of its own.

7. In Proverbs 3:5–6,

   Trust in the Lord with all your heart and lean not on your own understanding; in all your ways submit to him and he will make your paths straight.

Let Us Pray

Dear Lord, Savior of the world, hear my cry. Just like Faith in her story, I pray You give me strength and wisdom to not succumb to the tricks of the enemy. For evil comes in many different forms, and I rebuke it all in the name of Jesus! Grant me the vision I need to serve You, Lord. Draw me nearer to You. May you always dwell in me and my family. Your Word promised us that You will supply all my needs according to Your riches in glory. Lord, help me to believe and have faith in You and Your Word. You are my light in the darkness. You are my everything. Strengthen my faith as I learn to depend on You more and more each day and as You continue to walk with me. Thank You for Your grace and Your mercy. In Jesus Christ's name, I pray, amen!

Notes

_____
_____
_____
_____
_____
_____
_____
_____
_____
_____
_____
_____
_____
_____
_____
_____
_____
_____
_____
_____

IV

Patience

Patience was still a sophomore in high school when she got into a relationship with Bobbie, her then-acclaimed best friend and love of her life. With all sense of sincerity and genuineness, she desired the relationship to be everlasting. She wanted the togetherness, characterized by joy and happiness, to last a lifetime. Gentle Bobbie was entirely everything to her like no other guy had been. Nothing to them mattered more than being with each other. Wherever one went, the other one was right there.

She had wondered why Bobbie would be so fond of her. He has earned for himself the rare reputation of a celebrity. Having some pretty good artistic skills, he was then the spotlight for many ladies. Although not too tall, he had the kind of face that stopped you in your tracks. He was used to it—the sudden pause in people's natural expression when they looked his way followed by an incurious glance and a weak smile. Of course, the blush that accompanied it was a dead giveaway. It didn't help that he was so modest with it, and it made everyone fall for him even more. His soul was like that of an angel, and his heart like a lion's. He was slim and muscular with an almost symmetrical face.

It was at a birthday party earlier in her freshman year that she first met him, where Bobbie presented a solo song while playing the piano. He stunned all, including his soon-to-be lover. He was that inviting. Vanessa, her longtime friend who had invited her to the party, had an interest in him also. Apparently, although it did not seem he was commanding her attention, like a fruit seed, she would nurse this interest steadily and latently for a long time, aiming to eat from its fruit tree when fully mature.

Fifteen-year-old Patience had low self-esteem and suffered from depression because of her weight. Either she was too skinny because of her impromptu illnesses or she was overweight because she just loved food and couldn't control her mouth, but either way, she didn't like herself sometimes. She had a small circle of friends she would hang out with in school or after school, but she mostly was with her best friend, Vanessa, all the time. And after she met Bobbie at the party, she always questioned why her. With so many options from girls practically throwing themselves on him, he chose her. She didn't know if it was her witty and genuine personality that attracted him to her or if he was just trying to take advantage of her. Regardless of why it was that he liked her, she loved every bit of the attention he gave her. It made Patience feel like she was on cloud nine, and like never before, she felt wanted.

Patience had a horrible experience that promised to refresh itself in her memory because of its magnitude and intensity. Although, as a baby and young child, one needs a mother to be her keeper and a father to be her steadfast guide and role model, life just didn't unfold exactly that way for her. Patience had her earlier days under the watch of a strict dad. Her dad was always harsh and vehement with his countenance. In his chest beat a heart as noble as any fictional book heroes; he was one who would take untold hardships to honor the keeper of his soul.

Her mother was too beaten down, too emotionally crippled, to reflect even a fraction of the love needed to wrap up a growing child, as if she borrowed a leaf from her husband. Her father was so rigid that he kept strict discipline, never yielding, and was always in charge. The rules were the rules. Though her outside remained as beautiful as the day she first cried, her spirit struggled to survive in a world so cold and so bereft of love.

On the last day of classes during her freshman year of high school, Patience remembered it vividly—the scolding her dad gave her for not passing one of her classes according to his expectation. She had been feeling in her head something like the weight of her sins. She struggled alone with it, thinking it probably resulted from the bad nature of the conversation she had with her dad. The ache, however, heightened. She then thought it was because of hunger.

Suddenly, like thunder, a migraine struck, and Patience was its pitiful prisoner. Quite helpless in its cage, she was beginning to lose strength. She was getting blinded by flashing colorful spots and craved darkness, quiet, and stillness. The pain throbbed so violently around her skull that she thought it would crack open. It soon became a crushing pain on one side of her head that made her just walk around her room because she couldn't sit or lie down from the pain.

One eye was beginning to water on the painful side, and her nose became runny. She didn't know what was going on and didn't know what to think of herself. Her head throbbed, so she leaned it against the wall. Squeezing her eyes shut, she willed the pain to go away, but it wouldn't. She was getting detached from the rest of the world, and all her concentration was on the pain.

Suddenly, blood overcomes her. Real blood is nothing like movie blood. There is no amount of horror that can prepare a person for seeing so much blood exiting their own body, the hopelessness. She felt the blood run down her legs. Now she knew what was brewing in her. At the sight of this pool, Patience screamed. She had her final thoughts before everything eventually faded off. Death was not kind. Now Patience knew it. It snatched where it could, taking people who were far too young, far too beautiful. It didn't pretend to care; it didn't pretend to distinguish. The hooded vale of death now hung over her. It had never come that close, taking away all of her, seemingly, except for the mind that is still thinking. In fact, the body stopped feeling the palpitation.

Her mother ran to her aid once she heard the scream. She was in utter bafflement over what the ailment could be, so she rushed her to the hospital. Patience was admitted to the hospital and was being kept under observation for the bleeding. After many tests, she was referred to a specialist hospital, where efforts continued toward her understanding her ailment.

During those days while Patience was hospitalized, her mother, who had appeared to be emotionless while raising her children, became otherwise. She began to feel as if her life was being taken from her, as opposed to her baby girl's. Her heart was racing, and all she wanted to do was curl up into a ball, waiting for someone to wake her from this nightmare. But no one would. It seemed as if it was the end of the road for her.

Her father never saw something like that, even in his worst nightmares. And now he was seeing something his eyes won't ever be able to erase. His adrenaline flew over his veins like a carp through the river, but he couldn't move a single muscle, not even a scream would come out. The absolute horror completely paralyzed him, and the more he thought about it, the more he felt discouraged and utterly terrified. He didn't remember being that scared in his life.

Two days later, Patience was still in the hospital with very little information from the doctors. Her parents were still in a state of shock. The doctors carried out several tests and had finally drawn their conclusions about the cause of her bleeding. The doctors explained to her parents what was going on with the estrogen in her body. It caused the uterine lining to regenerate during each menstrual cycle and stimulated the growth of a fibroid in her uterus. "While she lost a lot of blood during this incident, she was going to be okay," was what was said, and she was discharged after a day of further observation.

Some hospital bills and tears of worry later, she continued to replay the memory in her head of what she saw before passing out. But she continued to nurse both the horror of the incident and the perpetuity of its occurrence. It was bound to happen again, just unknown when, so she was placed under serious medical watch. Patience hid her condition from everyone, including her boyfriend and best friend. She managed to escape from her friends and the outside world for seven to ten days every month while on her menstrual. It became the norm for Bobby and Vanessa. She avoided conversations about her time away from her friends.

It was becoming clearer to her and more obvious because her doctor verbalized to her that she would not be able to bear a child of her own. She became embarrassed of her situation and began to engage less with her family and friends. While Bobby's love for Patience did not change, he was pushed away by her as she remained distant. She went through life's journey with little contentment and resentment toward life, asking herself what she had done wrong to deserve what she was experiencing. For her, life would never get better, and nothing would ever go right. It didn't matter how many times her family and friends would tell her that if she thinks it, she will manifest it. She didn't believe in anything, especially old wives' tales, and she figured it was all going downhill anyway.

No matter the situations, the jobs, the friendships, the relationships, or the daydreams, Patience had lost her patience with life and everything and everyone in it. She lost faith in ever becoming a wife, a mother, a grandmother, a teacher, or a lover. She longed for one of the earth's happiest moments of being a woman. But she lost hope for it after years of being with Bobby and having no signs of pregnancy, which did not surprise her.

She could not see herself marrying Bobby because she thought it would be selfish of her not to share the beauty of childbirth with him. She also thought about the secret she kept from him all these years about her not being able to conceive. It tore her up inside, so instead of going on trying to keep a smile on her face, she felt it was best to leave him so he could make a family with someone else who would give that to him. She was heartbroken because she knew he was her soulmate. They always talked about getting married, but after years of keeping this secret from him, she felt horrible. She picked little things to argue about to sabotage the relationship and push him away. Bobby could not understand it, so he obliged. He stayed away.

Patience daydreamed about her wedding with Bobby and her children running around the house that they lived in outside of the city. She was startled by the ringing of her phone, and it was none other than the one she was thinking about. Despite the distance Patience tried to put between her and Bobby, he remained a phone call away. He called at least once a week to check up on her. They managed to still talk about marriage and the things they would do if they would end up being together again. And somehow, the conversation always turned into the number of kids that they wanted to have together. They talked all about how they would be as parents. She could hear the excitement in Bobby's voice when talking about it, and that was when her demeanor changed, and she tried to change the conversation to some gossip about Vanessa or some other mutual friend. Her sadness and self-consciousness triggered the gossip about others and fabricating stories to deflect from herself and her feelings.

Bobby surprised Patience with a trip to the Bahamas for her thirtieth birthday. They had the time of their lives there, and that's when Patience opened up to Bobby and told him about her condition and her barrenness. He professed his love for her and hugged her a little tighter. He apologized for being so insensitive and not knowing all those years. Even though it wasn't his fault that he didn't know why she kept pushing him away, he felt as if he could have tried a bit harder to get it out of her and reassure her that her feelings and secrets were safe with him. He always knew something was wrong but never really knew what it was. He reassured her this time that this would not change his love for her and that they can get through anything if they were together.

After their trip, Bobby was around more often, and they went on more and more dates. On one of those dates, Bobby decided to get down on one knee and pop the question. "Patience, will you marry me?" he asked with tears in his eyes. And with even more tears in her eyes, she excitedly screamed "Yes!" Patience could not believe her eyes as she gazed down at her engagement ring. She immediately went to those thoughts of what her wedding would be like. Bobby just smiled and stared at his beautiful fiancée standing in front of him.

A few months after the engagement, Bobby and Patience married at City Hall and moved in together. They talked about having a big wedding reception at a later date. Instead, they focused on what the doctor suggested to her regarding the possibility of conceiving. She underwent several surgeries to remove the fibroids; she had to increase the possibility of fertilization. After her last surgery with no complications, she fully recovered within two months, and she was ready to get back in the groove of things. Her doctor gave her hope. She would not give up after he assured her it would be a lot easier this time without the fibroids in the way. Her hope of pregnancy increased, and she began to erase the past from her memory.

But that couldn't have been further from the truth. Every month, she was a little more disappointed to find out that she still wasn't pregnant. She started to feel like a failure, and as the years went by, her husband started to get nervous that her biological clock was ticking. He was worried that, at this rate, she would run out of time to have a baby safely.

Five years later, she still wasn't pregnant. Even more devastating, the fibroids were back. This time, they brought shooting pain, heavy bleeding, and discomfort during intercourse. Her doctor told her that the fibroids were even larger and more aggressive than last time.

She had to have another surgery to remove all the fibroids. She couldn't stop the tears from falling in the doctor's office when she learned she would have another surgery. Not only was she worried about the scarring, but she also started to think that her reality was that she would never get to have a child.

The next three years were filled with a mix of emotions as her husband showered her with love, but she was longing for that other love. The love from a child. The sweetest love of all. She longed for the word *mommy* to be said to her.

Patience and Bobby began going to marriage counseling to help them cope with what was missing in their lives. Aside from that, they started attending a nearby church every Sunday. After forty years of life and feeling something was missing, they realized that void was Jesus Christ. They both gave their lives to Christ and lived their lives totally different from before. This time, Jesus Christ was at the center of all their decisions and prayers. They prayed together every morning and at night. They prayed that God would change their views of life and what was important. They prayed for forgiveness for wanting to change God's plan on how and when a child would enter their lives. They began to see life from a different perspective. They began serving the Lord at church and getting involved in one activity after another. They were so consumed with helping others that life was no longer just about them. Long gone were the days when they sat at home sobbing about not having a child of their own.

One day during service, the pastor announced to the congregation that a representative of the state's child protective services was going to be visiting the church to discuss the needs of the organization and how people could help. Among those needs was the adoption of children who have been in the foster care system for far too long. Patience and Bobby just turned to each other and smiled. They both thought it out loud, "Count us in!" A ray of light at the end of the tunnel was pierced through for them.

They attended the presentation and learned all about the adoption process and how they would be helping a child in need of a safe and loving home while at the same time filling that void of a child in their home. They were excited to get started on the process and get to know all about their new child. After months of interviews, home visits, inspections, and praying, they were blessed with a baby girl who had been abandoned by her parents at birth. After months of being in the system and no family members to claim her, six-month-old baby Eva found herself in the loving arms of Patience and Bobby.

Patience found her life's greatest and unexpected joy in Eva. Her thought alone, like an eraser, wiped away her pain from past years. Patience could do nothing but praise God for such a sudden change in life's course. The days ahead looked so much brighter.

Scripture Reflections

1. In Mark 5:34,

    He said to her, "Daughter, your faith has healed you. Go in peace and be freed from your suffering."

2. In James 5:8,

    You too, be patient and stand firm, because the Lord's coming is near.

3. In Romans 12:12,

    Be joyful in hope, patient in affliction, faithful in prayer.

4. In Philippians 4:6–7,

    Do not be anxious about anything, but in every situation, by prayer and petition, with thanksgiving, present your requests to God. And the peace of God, which transcends all understanding, will guard your hearts and your minds in Christ Jesus.

5. We may lose control, and fear may overcome us, but God is our strength since He is in control. In Psalm 73:26,

    My flesh and my heart may fail, but God is the strength of my heart and my portion forever.

6. In Psalm 37:5–7,

   Commit your way to the Lord; trust in him and he will do this: He will make your righteous reward shine like the dawn, your vindication like the noonday sun. Be still before the Lord and wait patiently for him; do not fret when people succeed in their ways, when they carry out their wicked schemes.

7. In Galatians 6:9,

   Let us not become weary in doing good, for at the proper time we will reap a harvest if we do not give up.

Let Us Pray

    Dear Lord, Savior of the world, hear my cry. Just like Patience in her story, I pray You come into my life and change my heart. Help me to wait patiently for You. Help me to seek Your face and to keep my eyes fixed on You. Help me to gain patience in all that I go through. For only You, Lord, will help me get through any trials and tribulations that come my way. For only You, O Lord, will lead the way and direct my paths. You are a waymaker and a miracle worker, and for that, I say thank You! For You, Lord, know the plans You have for me, plans to prosper me and not to harm me, plans to give me hope and a future. I trust in You, Lord, that You will grant the desires of my heart. Have Your way and will with me. Thank You for Your grace and Your mercy. In Jesus Christ's name, I pray, amen!

Notes

_____
_____
_____
_____
_____
_____
_____
_____
_____
_____
_____
_____
_____
_____
_____
_____
_____

V

Temperance

Temperance was at her usual biweekly manicure and pedicure appointment at the nail salon when she noticed something odd about her nail tech. She was not her cheery, perky self today. Temperance was being entertained by the nail tech's daughter while they carried on an animated conversation about her teachers in school. The girl was too smart for her own good, but she was a clown. She was mimicking her teacher and how she scolded her classmates for not completing their work. Temperance was laughing so hard that she found it quite difficult to keep still.

Things got quiet for a while when the little girl paused to catch her breath or probably think of something else silly to say. It was then Temperance had noticed the angry-looking bruise in the insides of her nail tech's arm. She had a fairly good guess of how it got there but asked regardless.

Her nail tech was a petite, good-looking young woman in her early thirties and was married with three children. Her daughter was rather outspoken and was quick to blurt, "My daddy beat her with his belt yesterday." She hushed the child hurriedly and, with an embarrassed smile, said, "Daddy didn't beat mommy, silly. He was only playing with me."

Her heart broke as she recognized in that instant that they were kindred spirits, partners in pain. She has also been down that road. It was sad to think that so many others are in the same situation but have no idea of what the next woman was going through. They all tried to hide it behind fake smiles and makeup. *How many more women are victims of domestic violence?* she asked herself.

She went into a daze and began thinking of her own situation and how it all started.

*****

Everything was going great. There was drinking and dancing. She just loved to dance. He knew how to charm her and get her attention. He had been different from all the rest in her life thus far. He listened to her, he loved her, and he changed her life. Temperance felt like she owed him the world for all that he had done for her the past few months. This man had been helping her get her life back in order, and they learned all about each other's lives in a small amount of time. She owed him a lot, but she wasn't sure if what she experienced that night was supposed to happen or be excused. He told her to relax and that he would never hurt her. He looked her in the eyes and told her how beautiful she was as they danced. She smiled shyly with her head down. With one hand, he lifted her head, and with the other, he grabbed her hand. He whispered, "It's okay. I won't ever hurt you." He leaned forward and kissed her lips. Her heartbeat was so fast she thought she would faint. She wasn't ready to give in to him just yet, but she felt he would be disappointed if she didn't.

All Temperance knew was that she loved this man. He was her everything. One bad relationship after another, she thought she had finally found the one. He was everything the others weren't. In past relationships, she was the domineering one, but the tables turned in this new love.

It all started with flowers, dates, and gifts—expensive ones! She never experienced this type of love before. It's like he knew everything she needed and wanted. He was there to provide it to her. She felt indebted to him for loving her the way he did. Things were far too good to be true. It was only a few months into the relationship, and that night, he forced her to do things with him against her will. Things she could not imagine doing ever.

She became another person she didn't even recognize. She crawled into bed, hugged her pillow tight, and cried as if tomorrow would never come. The next day, he came by her place to see her, and she was still in bed and refused to see him. Her relationship with him had affected her everyday life.

Her best friend was a party animal just like she was when in her twenties, but this wasn't the case anymore. Those days for Temperance were over. She had outgrown that stage in her life. She would rather stay at home reading books and listening to music now. Her bestie would many times complain that Temperance led a boring life now and that she was dull and needed to get out more like she used to.

One day, she succeeded in getting her to dress up and follow her to a party. While there, she sat, looking around and observing. It was obvious that she would rather be somewhere else, but then a charming and sophisticated man walked up to her and kept her company throughout the night. He was quite the intellectual, an avid reader like herself, and they had a very nice time discussing the books they had read. They exchanged numbers and promised to stay in touch. They went on dates frequently, and she started going over to his place to spend weekends. It was absolutely amazing and exhilarating to fall in love again. Things looked so perfect that it seemed nearly impossible for anything to go wrong.

The cracks started to appear, and the plaster started falling off the walls of their relationship. He started finding fault with what she did and grew overly critical of her. As for him, he could do no wrong. Everything he did and said was right. He persuaded her to move in with him. He had a way of making things she found out seem like they weren't true. Outside, he seemed like the perfect partner, and people were naturally attracted to him. He was overly critical of her friends and family. She eventually cut ties with everyone around her because of him and was isolated. He became irrationally jealous, obsessive, and accusatory. She could hardly concentrate on her work because he would call her countless times when she was at work and get upset and start yelling at her if she didn't get home at the usual time. She hardly had any freedom. He was at the helm of her life, and she felt choked.

She would boil inwardly whenever he berated her, but on this particular day, she had enough of him and could no longer tolerate his verbal abuse, so she yelled right back at him. He lost it and beat her beyond consciousness. When she woke up, she saw him at her bedside, apologizing furiously and begging her not to leave, saying he didn't know what came over him and swore not to beat her again. She gave him another chance, but things only deteriorated further. He even started hitting her when they were in public. He seized her phone and prevented her from attending gatherings on some occasions. She feared for her life. She foolishly threatened to leave him, and she was beaten up again. He threatened to hunt her down and repossess her wherever she went as she was his until he no longer wanted her. She put up with his madness a little longer and a day, not caring what would happen to her next.

She placed a call to her sister and told her of the grave danger she was in. She reasoned that being dead was far better than the way she was living. Her sister wasted no time and swung immediately into action. She hid at a friend of her sister's and went back accompanied by the police to pack her belongings. He was arrested and put behind bars. However, soon after, he made bail and was released. Fearing for her life, she left town, abandoning her job and the life she had created for herself back home. She found a new job at a restaurant and lived a low profile for a year until her sister was able to scrape some money together to help her get her own place.

She moved on with her life and got a second job to occupy her time and mind. She didn't have anyone to entertain, so she spent most of her time working and saving money. She totally avoided dating and relationships because she remembered what she faced in the past. As much as she avoided men, she loved children and wanted to have her own family. She wanted to be loved and appreciated—just not that way. She realized that was not love.

A coworker invited her to attend church with her one Sunday, and she agreed since she had the day off. Temperance was not a churchgoing person at all. As she walked into the church, all she could think about was her past and all the sinful acts she had done. She felt judged; she felt as if everyone was staring at her. She was uncomfortable and wanted to get out of there fast. She turned to her coworker, gave her a smile, and told her to relax and that everything was going to be fine. "Listen, Temperance," she said. "Everyone has a past, and everyone has sinned, so don't beat yourself up. We have no authority to judge you."

Temperance just looked at her and squinted her eyes as if to say "Yeah, okay."

As she stepped into the pew, she looked over at where the cameras were facing, where she noticed a tall, handsome man staring at her as she took her seat. He winked at her! "Did he just wink at me in church?" She wondered. She smirked and put her head down. She ignored his gesture to catch his attention. But she asked her coworker for the scoop on him.

Temperance began to frequent the church. One day, she was introduced to the head of the media crew, which happens to be the same person who winked at her on her first day there. His name was Jacob and seemed like a nice young man. He said he loved God and was devoted to church and his service there. They became friends and began dating. She started to unveil and confessed about her past. She told him how she had been hurt in a previous relationship. He comforted her and assured her of better days. He had no real job yet, but the church was paying him a stipend for his service. But Temperance didn't care about that. She saw past that. Something was different about this one.

Things were going good for a few months, and the conversations began to include marriage plans. She knew it was too soon to talk about that, but she went along with his ideas until he brought up a business plan that required her to lend him the money to fund it. She was wiser now and turned him down. She noticed a change in his behavior, and several weeks after, he brought up the issue again. She still refused, and instead of backing down, he beat her down and forced her to sign some papers; she had no clue what she was signing for. He was later arrested, and the loan was overturned, but she never got over it.

She became depressed and attempted to kill herself by overdosing on sleeping pills. It was a trying time for her older sister as she stayed with her through the whole healing process and rehabilitation.

Those days were completely bleak and dark. She saw no point in living. Everyone she loved had taken advantage of her. Maybe she was the problem, and there was something wrong with her that made them treat her awfully. She questioned herself. She loathed herself and desperately sought to end it all until a group of students from the hospital fellowship paid her a visit. They shared the gospel of Christ and prayed with her. On the way out, one of them hugged her and whispered in her ear, "Jesus loves you." She broke down and wept.

Where was Jesus when her parents died in an accident? Where was He when her aunt treated her like a slave? Where was His love all those years she tried to be good and do right? Where was He when people took advantage of her? She knew she had sinned, but hadn't she suffered enough? They used to tell her God was merciful, yet no one had shown her any form of mercy. She looked to the pills again to get her through the night.

She later enrolled in a Christian women's domestic abuse program, and she heard other women share their stories, some of which were far worse than hers. In one of those meetings, she made her peace with God and was convinced of His love for her. As for herself, she had the rest of her life to make peace with herself. She dropped all the guilt, pain, and betrayal at the feet of Jesus. She now had his love and forgiveness. If Jesus could forgive her, she had to forgive herself for her actions and thinking.

She really loved Jesus and wanted to help others see His love also, so she started on the long, hard journey of learning to love herself even with her faults, shortcomings, and imperfections. She realized that failure to do so would make her vulnerable to becoming an object of abuse and predators again. She clung to the words and truth of the scripture as the truths about her life, and gradually, she developed a positive view of herself, believing the words of God as the only enduring and unchangeable truth.

The Holy Spirit emboldened her by the day such that she found herself doing things she never thought of doing. Even her stuttering and nervousness around people were gone. She spent the rest of her coming years reaching out to women and children who were victims of abuse. She found her calling, her purpose.

Scripture Reflections

1. In Galatians 5:22–23,

    But the fruit of the Spirit is love, joy, peace, forbearance, kindness, goodness, faithfulness, gentleness and self-control. Against such things there is no law.

2. In 1 Peter 1:13–16,

    Therefore, with minds that are alert and fully sober, set your hope on the grace to be brought to you when Jesus Christ is revealed at his coming. As obedient children do not conform to the evil desires you had when you lived in ignorance. But just as he who called you is holy, so be holy in all you do; for it is written: "Be holy, because I am holy."

3. In Ephesians 4:1–3,

    As a prisoner for the Lord, then, I urge you to live a life worthy of the calling you have received. Be completely humble and gentle; be patient, bearing with one another in love. Make every effort to keep the unity of the Spirit through the bond of peace.

4. In John 14:27,

    Peace I leave with you; my peace I give you. I do not give to you as the world gives. Do not let your hearts be troubled and do not be afraid.

5. In Romans 5:1–5,

Therefore, since we have been justified through faith, we have peace with God through our Lord Jesus Christ, through whom we have gained access by faith into this grace in which we now stand. And we boast in the hope of the glory of God. Not only so, but we also glory in our sufferings, because we know that suffering produces perseverance; perseverance, character; and character, hope. And hope does not put us to shame, because God's love has been poured out into our hearts through the Holy Spirit, who has been given to us.

6. In Psalm 4:1,

Answer me when I call to you, my righteous God. Give me relief from my distress; have mercy on me and hear my prayer.

7. In Romans 8:28–30,

And we know that in all things God works for the good of those who love him, who have been called according to his purpose. For those God foreknew he also predestined to be conformed to the image of his Son, that he might be the firstborn among many brothers and sisters. And those he predestined, he also called; those he called, he also justified; those he justified, he also glorified.

Let Us Pray

Dear Lord, Savior of the world, hear my cry. Just like Temperance in her story, I pray for Your healing power. I pray that You will lift me and separate me from the burden of hurt feelings of the past. Help me to get beyond yesterday's upset thoughts. I pray that You remove all my despair and release all my concerns. The feelings of sadness are behind me, and your powerful presence surrounds me, governing every situation in my life. Lord, help me to let go and let You take over! I know that when I do this, You open doors of endless possibilities and joy. Change me, O Lord, and allow me to forgive those who have hurt me. Thank You for bringing me through. Thank You for the breakthrough. Thank You for Your grace and Your mercy. In Jesus Christ's name, I pray, amen!

Notes

VI

Justice

Glancing at his watch, David saw that it was a quarter past one. He was supposed to meet a group of twelve freshmen at the covered pavilion near the school library to help prepare them for a debate. He noticed how they sat dumbstruck in awe of him. He wasn't so comfortable with them having to gaze up at him, so he suggested that they moved to an expanse of lawn not far away.

He picked up their discussion where they had left off at their last meeting. A few minutes later, the missing ones arrived. David gave a frown of disapproval; he did not quite tolerate tardiness in any form. The two guys entering seemed more interested in the girl who was walking in late with them than in the subject of discussion David had going on. Another girl was looking at David with a decided gleam in her eyes. He kept the tutorial to an hour and a half and ended it by telling them to enjoy their weekend. He picked out materials for them to study and several questions to think about before the next meeting. Then he dismissed them. The girl who had been eyeing him quickly took her chance. She tried making small talk with him about what they were discussing at the meeting, but he had a feeling she wasn't concentrating on his answers.

"It's all very interesting, but I'm still not clear about several things you said." She looked up at him. "Maybe we could talk more about it at your place? I would ask you to mine, but I have a roommate, and the place is always a mess." She smiled. "I could bring some wine."

"I don't think that would be a good idea," snapped David as he collected his books.

"The wine or coming to your apartment?" she asked, with a smirk on her face.

"Both!" he replied.

She widened her eyes. "Why not?"

"I have a girlfriend."

She laughed. "I don't bite, I promise!"

He stopped and faced her. "You would try, and this needs to stop!"

She reached out and ran a finger down his chest, whispering in his ear, "I like a challenge."

He swallowed with difficulty. She was pretty, had a very nice body, and was willing. A few years back, he would have gladly jumped at the invitation, but now he couldn't even entertain the thoughts. He promised Justice he would be good; he knew he hurt her before for which he was very sorry. He loved her and couldn't bear the thought of losing her, which might become a reality if she ever caught wind of his unfaithfulness. He was used to situations like this, ladies coming on to him. He reminded himself daily that he was responsible for his choices and that he was not going to cheat. He stayed that way for a while before lust got the best of him again, and he stumbled down the familiar rocky road.

After fifteen years, David and his girlfriend, Justice, were still together because Justice refused to ever consider splitting up despite David's unfaithfulness during most of their time together.

They met at the university, and he was all the classic things: tall, good-looking, bright, and funny. Very few women could resist him, not excusing him for the immeasurable pain he has caused her, but she made up her mind to stick through with the relationship wherever it ends.

He was a very popular figure on campus. Not only was he on the basketball team and had won major victories for the school, but he was also on the school's debate team and was well-known for his oratory skills. He was quite the A-lister as he was also one of the best students.

It was at a freshman welcome party that they first laid eyes on each other. For Justice, it was love at first sight, but her conversation starter and body language challenged David to make her feel like she was the only person in the room with him. Little did she know that he had already gathered a few other phone numbers prior to laying eyes on her. And Justice already had one in her pocket from a previous conversation she had with someone else she met before meeting David.

Justice, who was already having designs on David, seized her chance and played the lie to her advantage. She made fast moves on him, and they began dating each other within a matter of days. She really liked him and would do anything to keep him. She didn't see any wrong in what she did. It was called "acting smart." Besides, David was very cool with it.

Justice was from a wealthy family while David was from an average home. She shared whatever she had with him, and he helped her with difficult schoolwork. Then he had gotten popular, and the girls were attracted to him as if drawn by a magnet. Many girls liked the idea of being seen with him, not worrying about a girlfriend. They looked for the association of this handsome man.

Because of his leadership positions, he had to interact with many girls some of which would try to force themselves on him. At first, he practiced a great deal of self-restraint, but after a while, he got tired of being called soft by his peers. The girls didn't make it any easier saying he was inexperienced and dull. The pressure was mounting, and temptation grew by the day from the daughters of Eve until his restraint broke.

It was this girl or that one or any girl that made herself available. Such was the life of a basketball jockey. He could have any girl he wanted at the snap of his fingers. He used them mostly for pleasure and nothing else. It was Justice he really cared for, and he went to great lengths to keep his double life away from her because she would be deeply hurt and broken. Truthfully speaking, it was the normal thing among his teammates to keep multiple girls around; they saw absolutely nothing wrong with it. Discussions held were mainly regarding girls and booze and more girls and booze.

Justice had been hearing the rumors about her boyfriend but wouldn't believe them. Rumors about how he had multiple girls in the locker room and in his car. Girls would always talk, and somehow it ended in her ears. She became depressed and constantly asked herself why wasn't she enough for him. She saw and learned quite a lot when growing up about cheating men who she thought would attract something different and find a guy who was caring, loving, devoted, and hers alone. However, history was repeating itself again. She thought he was different. "What is wrong with men?" She was terribly confused as to what to do with the information she heard and didn't quite know how to confront him.

One day, she pretended to be a little drunk and asked him if he was being unfaithful to her. He stared at her shocked and dismayed and asked why she would even think of such a thing as he would never do that.

She was relieved for a while before the rumors started again, but this time, she was going to find out on her own, consequences be damned. She got her hands on his phone while he was deep asleep. He had recently returned from an interschool competition and was gone for three days. She found implicating text messages between him and a female student at the school. They planned to get together even before he traveled and had been with her when he wasn't in training.

She returned the phone to its normal position and asked him about it the next morning. He had denied it completely, and she would have believed him if she hadn't seen the evidence with her own eyes. He made it look as if she was cooking up stories or was rather crazy. That hurt more than the betrayal. Feeling confused and disillusioned, she stormed out in anger. He felt like a total jerk, but it was an unspoken rule that even if you were caught in the act, you will still have to deny it.

For men, admitting that you cheated was more of a sin than cheating itself. She refused to talk to him or even see him for the rest of the semester and did not pick up his calls even when he had called a hundred times a day. He did everything humanly possible to get back in her good graces, but hell has no greater fury than a woman scorned. She had sworn never to have anything to do with him or any other member of the male species on campus, but who was she deceiving? The next session, they were back together again after he had signed an agreement to be on his best behavior. The agreement only lasted for two months before he was back to his philandering ways again.

Then the rumors started again. This time, she made up her mind to catch him in the very act. So after he escorted her to her house one night and he turned around, she followed him at a distance. She saw him go into a bar and, minutes later, walk out with a girl on his arm, and they both walked to his apartment. Her curiosity fled at once and was replaced with a sick feeling. She leaned over the sidewalk and threw up. Her legs gave way underneath her, and she sat there crying. After what seemed like hours, she stood up, walked up to his door, and knocked. When she heard that the approaching footsteps were quite close, she turned her back and walked away. She wanted to just let him know that she knew what he was up to.

Their relationship was an endless cycle of cheating, breaking up, and reconciling. And before they knew it, college was over. They had gone their separate ways, David to law school and Justice to a culinary institute. They dated on and off for five years. He went on to work for a big law firm while she baked in the comforts of her kitchen. He became quite wealthy and was very generous to her. He took her on vacations and spoiled her with many gifts. He flew into town to see her twice a month.

On their tenth anniversary of being together, he had taken her on a trip to Hawaii where he proposed. He was a busy man and quite ambitious, so he had planned to make partner at the law firm in the future and was working furiously to achieve it. Therefore, he wasn't quite ready to settle down yet but felt like it was what Justice needed and wanted. However, he very much enjoyed his freedom and spending time with all the beautiful women in his life.

His engagement didn't put a halt to his promiscuity, aided by the fact that they were in a long-distance relationship. It was like the tale of the leopard that couldn't wash off his spots. He knew how to play his game well if he practiced his infidelity far away from his girlfriend. That was what being the man was about.

Justice was growing restless again; she wondered what being married to David would look like. Would getting married make him quit cheating? She knew about his affairs and escapades. She knew he was no saint but felt rather at a loss. He was caring, gentle, loving, attentive, and still the most charming. He was also very generous to her and her family. He made sure that she didn't lack anything and practically put his wallet at her disposal. He took her out with him and introduced her to everyone and anyone who mattered.

Everyone knew that they were engaged, but there were still wild rumors of his other life, which he always tried to shield her from. She understood that none of the other women mattered, but she still couldn't come to terms with his cheating no matter how many times she would come up with excuses for him. She would, at times, blame herself for his actions, easily forgiving him or sometimes deciding to leave him for good.

Her mother had told her from experience "that all men are the same. Just pick yourself a good one." So she was scared to let go of what she had for fear of finding someone worse.

In the end, she reasoned that he really loved her as he was never serious with the other women, and with time, she would nurse him to faithfulness with patience on her part.

She decided to be happy and make the best use of life as she experienced it. Life is too short to live in misery because of a cheating partner. She would look the other way, and doing so kept her sanity at peace.

Their fifteenth anniversary was drawing close and their wedding plans even closer. He was seldom at home but made it up to her in many ways. She spent her days doing serious shopping and making delicacies. It didn't matter that her husband-to-be was sleeping with the event planner or that he was constantly after anything in skirts. She chose to be happy, and nothing would take that from her.

She began to pray for her life and what was to come of it once married. She asked God for forgiveness and prayed for her and David's salvation. She also prayed the serenity prayer out loud every night for her peace: *"God, grant me the serenity to accept the things I cannot change, courage to change the things I can, and wisdom to know the difference."*

Scripture Reflections

1. Confess your sins and errors to the Lord for forgiveness and mercy. In Proverbs 28:13,

    Whoever conceals their sins does not prosper, but the one who confesses and renounces them finds mercy.

2. Uphold us by your righteousness so that we will not stumble unto destruction and calamity. In James 3:2,

    Not many of you should become teachers, my fellow believers, because you know that we who teach will be judged more strictly. We all stumble in many ways. Anyone who is never at fault in what they say is perfect, able to keep their whole body in check.

3. In John 14:1,

    Do not let your hearts be troubled. You believe in God; believe also in me.

4. In Isaiah 59:1–4,

    Surely the arm of the Lord is not too short to save, nor his ear too dull to hear. But your iniquities have separated you from your God; your sins have hidden his face from you, so that he will not hear. For your hands are stained with blood, your fingers with guilt. Your lips have spoken falsely, and your tongue mutters wicked things. No one calls for justice; no one pleads a case with integrity. They rely on empty arguments, they utter lies; they conceive trouble and give birth to evil.

5. In 2 Timothy 2:22–26,

   Flee the evil desires of youth and pursue righteousness, faith, love and peace, along with those who call on the Lord out of a pure heart. Don't have anything to do with foolish and stupid arguments, because you know they produce quarrels. And the Lord's servant must not be quarrelsome but must be kind to everyone, able to teach, not resentful. Opponents must be gently instructed, in the hope that God will grant them repentance leading them to a knowledge of the truth, and that they will come to their senses and escape from the trap of the devil, who has taken them captive to do his will.

6. In Psalm 139:14,

   I praise you because I am fearfully and wonderfully made; your works are wonderful, I know that full well.

7. In Romans 10:9–10,

   If you declare with your mouth, "Jesus is Lord," and believe in your heart that God raised him from the dead, you will be saved. For it is with your heart that you believe and are justified, and it is with your mouth that you profess your faith and are saved.

Let Us Pray

Dear Lord, Savior of the world, hear my cry. Just like Justice in her story, I pray for Your joy and Your peace. Help me to see my worth and value myself as such. Open my eyes to see what I truly deserve. Allow me to forgive others for their misdoings against me and also to know the difference between accepting and tolerating their behaviors. Show me clarity. Give me the discernment to see those who belong in my life to elevate me and draw me closer to them. At the same time, reveal those who need to be removed and help me step away from them. Renew my strength and allow me to move forward in You. Thank You for all You have done and continue to do in my life. Thank You for Your grace and Your mercy. In Jesus Christ's name, I pray, amen!

Notes

VII

Love

It was the question Love waited so long to hear. She dreamed of this day and envisioned it in her head but never knew exactly how it would actually turn out. Jonah and Love had just finished eating a delicious meal at a fancy restaurant when he took her hand and looked intently into her eyes. She thought to herself, *Did I really hear those words, or are my ears deceiving me?* She was too overwhelmed by emotions to answer.

Puzzled at her silence, he asked again, this time, shaking her hand, "Love, will you marry me?" Even then, no words were uttered out of her mouth, so she just nodded frantically with a huge smile. Finally! She yelled out, "Yes! Yes! Yes, I'll marry you!" as he slipped the ring on her finger. He stood up and pulled her up to kiss him amidst the clapping and the whooping of onlookers. With mascara dripping down her face from her tears, she smiled with no care in the world. The day had finally come. She was engaged to the one man who had her heart for the past fifteen years. She would never forget that beautiful evening.

After three children together and the devastation of multiple breakups in between, Love thought to herself, *Who else could I end up married to?* Love was determined to make this relationship work, and her biggest fear was adding to the statistics of being a single mother. She would not allow anything or anyone to get in her way of marrying the father of her children, or so she thought.

Fifteen years prior

    Jonah and Love separately attended a party and were introduced to each other by a mutual friend. They hit it off almost immediately. Jonah was full of charms, handsome, tall, smart, and funny. What more could a woman want? He was quite a tempting morsel. They exchanged numbers, and before they knew it, they were deep into conversations with each other. He was the type of guy women felt safe around, the macho type. Whenever they went out together, other women were obviously eyeing him, and she felt like the prize winner. "Sorry," she would say with her eyes, "this one's mine." Indeed, she was a lucky woman. He always treated her like royalty and bought her things that she would never imagine having or getting for herself. He made her feel special in every way. They talked on the phone for hours about their family dynamics, their goals, and aspirations, and even all the things he wanted to do for her. She's never been this vulnerable before, and she was open to doing anything and everything with Jonah.

    Things were fantastic between them for a year after which they started making plans toward a more serious and committed relationship. They were planning on starting a home together, the kind with flowers, a garden, and babies running around. Love worked for a law firm at that time and was quite successful for a young woman in her twenties. He, on the other hand, had his own business that was not quite successful. Yet he looked promising even though her parents wouldn't approve of him.

    She had dreams of getting married, building a large empire together, and having children. They purchased a home together a year into their relationship, and it wasn't exactly as she dreamed, but it would do quite alright. He still hadn't proposed or said anything about marriage, but Love was happy and confident that he would one day.

    Shortly after moving into their new home, Love discovered she was pregnant. Her joy knew no bounds. She loved this man with her whole heart and was happy to have his baby. These were the happiest times of her life. He was caring and dutiful, treated her like a queen, and paid her lots of attention. She felt more than fortunate to have him even though he had not yet proposed. She was living in a bubble.

When baby Jonah Jr., or JJ as they called him, was born, she could literally see the pride shining in his eyes as he welcomed their little one into the world. It was a difficult labor, and he stayed with her the entire time, holding her hands, whispering words of encouragement, wiping away perspiration from her forehead, and smoothing her hair; he was her angel and protector.

After the baby was born, he provided all the help and assistance Love required. A few weeks after, JJ was crying a lot, and Jonah said he wanted to clear his head. Love understood him quite well as the baby's cry and many sleepless nights were driving both her and Jonah crazy. All she thought was that he was merely going on a short drive because she saw him take his car keys. He was gone for hours. She was getting really upset as the night went on, and the baby's crying only got worse. She dialed his phone many times on end, but it would go straight to voicemail.

When he finally returned, it was after midnight, and he dished her a not-very-well-cooked story and took the baby from her, who then calmed down and fell asleep almost immediately. She was mad and glad at the same time; however, there was this uncomfortable feeling in her that what he was saying to her was a lie, and she chose to ignore it though.

The same situation repeated itself several times. He was suddenly meeting with some unknown business partners at odd hours and staying away from home longer than usual. She was worried, but when she confronted him, he would assure her that everything was okay. She just knew he was lying to her but couldn't prove it just yet. They started having some minor issues and quarrels. He was no longer assisting her with the baby as he used to, and he said that she was neglecting him. She had no idea what the real issue was, nor did she expect her bubble to burst.

One day, a friend of hers told her she had spotted Jonah with another young lady at a restaurant, and that got her quite unsettled, but instead of asking him, she chose to do investigations of her own. Her days of confusion ended when another one of her friends brought her a stunning revelation. A friend of the friend had been going on and on about some wonderful new guy she had been dating who later turned out to be Jonah when she was shown a picture. Love was totally devastated. She couldn't believe she had been so clueless. Her head hurt for days. He told the other lady that he was seeing someone presently, but they had serious issues and were about to break it off.

 She did not confront him immediately; she waited a few days since she was in denial and desperately wanted to believe that the story wasn't true. His seemingly honest eyes bored into hers as if trying to convince her he was not lying, despite having her evidence. She found it too hard. He would seem so honest and telling that she was almost persuaded to believe him. His quivering lips begged her to believe him even against the evidence. Going through his phone while he was asleep further gave her solid proof of what she had already discovered and pulled the last layer of wool from over her eyes. She was utterly devastated! She had put the entirety of herself into the relationship, and she was played for a fool. She no longer wanted to confront him. She just wanted out.

 Being one prone to react, she began the proceedings of leaving the relationship and the house before confronting him. Seeing boxes being filled up every day, he denied every single bit of the accusations. He even got angry and put up a scene like she had gone crazy and didn't know what she was talking about. She would have probably believed him if she had not seen for herself what he was capable of, and the fact that he denied it hurt the most.

 Lies can put one off balance and make you crazy and sick to your stomach; that was exactly what they did to Love. She could not continue to stay with someone who was not only a cheater but also a prolific liar, so she scraped whatever little savings she had after leaving her house behind and secured an apartment out of town with her baby.

 She had to look for a job to pay her bills and take care of JJ. He was the only bright spot in her life during those trying periods, so she showered him with all the love she had in her heart. Getting a new job was not easy, but she persevered. Bills were piling up because of credit card debt she could not afford to pay on her own since Jonah would mainly take care of those payments in the past. With the house and cars being in her name and all the credit card debt, she was drowning in; she had no choice but to file for bankruptcy. Doing that allowed her to rewrite her financial story. Things were looking a bit better for Love and JJ after a year of leaving Jonah. Nonetheless, he was still around visiting JJ and trying to reignite a flame that would not turn back on. She started attending a community church where she made friends who would try to guide her on the right path.

One day, Jonah went back unexpectedly and said he wanted to talk. He was saying how sorry he was for hurting her, but she wasn't buying it. She later learned that his girlfriend had dumped him when she found out the truth. He kept going back every day until Love finally agreed to allow him to step foot into her new place. The actual truth was that she was not as immune to his charms as she thought she was. Her insides practically fell to mush each time she saw him. He apologized for his past mistakes, and that was it; things were gradually going back to the way they were between them before, and she decided to give him a second chance since he seemed to have changed. They reconciled, and he moved in with her and JJ again. If only she had known that she was setting herself up for a vicious cycle of heartbreak and frustration.

Not long after his return, she discovered she was pregnant again, only this time she did not give up her job or entertain any silly notion. Jonah was really applying himself to fatherhood and being a good partner, and they were making progress in their relationship, or so she thought. Not long after her second baby, Noah, was born, she discovered that he had been cheating on her with one of his childhood friends. She was done! She packed his bags, put them outside, and didn't let him inside her apartment anymore.

The following year, she and the kids moved to a larger and more decent accommodation. Love thought about going out into the dating scene and meeting new people since it seemed like it was never going to work out with Jonah. As part of her search for single guys, she took it to social media to befriend others and rekindle friendships from the past. During one of her searches, she found her childhood friend whom she had not seen since middle school. They messaged each other, met up, went on a few dates, and hit it off nicely. At the same time, however, Jonah was still around looking to spend time with his children and "family."

Jonah, after three months of being around, came back with his apologies, and to everyone's surprise, Love took him back in. She didn't want to be a single mother taking care of two kids all alone since she didn't think any other man would want her with kids. To his credit, he was a terrific dad, and his children adored him. They began talking about buying a new home and making plans to move out of the city and into the suburbs for a better life for their children. At this point, Love had forgotten all about the people she met during her dating sprint and the good times she had with her childhood friend.

Once again, she got pregnant. This time, she wasn't so quick to tell him because she wasn't sure if this was the right move to make with him after their previous breakups and hiccups. And just when she decided to tell him, he told her there was something very important he had to tell her. By the look on his face, she was going to be heartbroken again. She told him to spit it out already. With tears in his eyes, he confessed to Love that he had a baby with another girl, and it had happened while they were on a break. So while Love was pregnant with her third child, he was already the father to his third child who was born months prior.

She couldn't comprehend. Love was terribly shaken up; the painful reality of the whole situation dawned on her. She was depressed and considered terminating her pregnancy. She didn't know what to do: abort or continue with the pregnancy. She prayed about it and decided to keep her baby. She didn't want to change her life plans because of someone else's plans and mistakes. Love was determined to buy her home with Jonah and live a different life in the suburbs with him and their children. So she did just that shortly after. They purchased their new home as they had planned.

Still pregnant, Love and Jonah moved into the new home with their two kids. The rest of the year after the birth of the third child was uneventful. The kids were trying to adjust to their new environment, and Love had her hands quite full with taking care of the baby while still working full-time.

Everything seemed to be going well until Jonah began his late-night rendezvous and long drives to nowhere. That was how she was able to confront him on his cheating, again! Love no longer had any strength left in her for accusations and quarrels, so she simply asked him to leave after she packed his bags, yet again! He did just that with no problem.

After not seeing him for months, she noticed a different type of swagger during his visit with the kids. It seemed like he ran into some money because there was a cockiness that was evident in his manner. The children were happy to see him, however, and he found his way back into their lives, again!

This time around, Love was tired already. She didn't care anymore what he did with himself. He could jump off a cliff for all she cared. She had lost interest in the relationship and only wanted to live her life in peace and take care of her kids. She was tired of the frustration, disappointment, pain, and hurt, and of hoping that he was going to turn a new leaf, which she knew was a lie. He hurt her one too many times before. She took all she could take. They maintained a civil relationship because of the kids, but they were practically housemates as they couldn't even bear having to sleep in the same room together, so she began sleeping in another bedroom.

Jonah would try to show her that he was now a changed man, but Love wasn't buying it. Only a fool keeps falling for the same tricks over and over. Her momma certainly didn't raise no fool. She ignored all his attempts to work his way back into her heart, and certainly all his apologies. He was asking for a clean slate, a fresh start, but Love wasn't going to be played for the fool again.

Jonah tried a different angle. He started with small gifts, notes, flowers, and other romantic gestures. Love felt he would realize the foolishness of it all and quit his acting. He was acting weird, treating her the way he used to in their early days, taking her on dinner dates and the movies. But her mind wasn't at rest. She couldn't help but wonder if he was on to some mischief again. She couldn't figure it out, but he kept acting this way for a long time that Love started considering a change of heart. She let him back in yet again!

That's when he officially proposed to Love after fifteen years of being together, on and off, of course.

*****

She didn't know she could cry so much. All the years of pain, hurt, disappointment, and suffering faded in that instant. Yes, she screamed out to him after the awkward silence. This was for life this time. She couldn't believe it!

Well, Love lived in her fantasy world for two months when he told her that he had a confession to make since they had agreed to be honest with each other from now on. He told her that while on their last break from each other, he was seeing someone, and that person claimed to be pregnant by him, and he wanted to be sure if he was the father. She became quite suspicious, so she asked a reliable source to check out his story with his other friends and family.

Later while she waited to confirm if the pregnancy allegation was true, the reliable source uncovered another one of his ugly secrets. The other woman had already given birth to his baby a few months prior to him telling Love that it might be his baby she was pregnant with. To top it off, he was in the delivery room with her when she gave birth. This was the last straw that broke the camel's back.

Love now saw this man for who he really was. She wasn't sad; instead, she went crazy. She thought to herself, *How could I have allowed someone to bring so much misery into my life?* She wasted so many years on continuous cycles of heartbreak, disappointment, and deceit. Love was quite surprised to still have her sanity.

She packed up his belongings and demanded him to leave immediately, but he had the guts to refuse after all he put her through. There, she lost her temper and got into a shouting match that didn't solve anything either. He still refused to go. She realized the situation was way beyond what she could handle. She needed to take drastic measures if she really wanted him out of her life.

After a few more months of putting up with his nonsense and getting sick and tired of him, she decided to take matters into her own hands. While he was out one day, she knocked his room door down and, like a mad woman, began to pack all his belongings in black garbage bags. She was getting closer to being free, and she did not shed one tear as she packed. She was not going to allow anyone to force her to live with them if she didn't want to. She was sick and tired of being sick and tired. By the evening, all twenty bags were on the driveway, and the locks to all the doors were changed.

To his surprise, he was unable to unlock the door when he returned to the house. He banged on the door and called Love's phone nonstop. She did not know what was going to happen next.

Though she thought to herself that she won, the victory felt quite empty. It was like a drop in the ocean when compared with the trauma she went through. Love couldn't stop imagining how her life might have taken a different path had she not been fortunate enough to meet Jonah. She was drained financially, emotionally, and spiritually. She was drained of life itself. How could she waste her one chance at life like this? She was depressed for months, and the drive to keep at anything was gone. Her job suffered, but the kids suffered the most. She was an emotional wreck. Eventually, she was forced to see a therapist, but that became expensive, so she stopped going after two sessions.

She turned to the one she had been turning to for the past fifteen years, her Lord and Savior. She had forgotten, however, about the power of prayer and repentance. Love grew up going to church with her mom and grandparents as a little girl, and she loved it, but she stopped going as an adult. Even though she thought of going occasionally, Jonah was never too keen about church, and he had some twisted thoughts, so she did not make it her business to attend while dating him. All Love wanted to do was make him happy, so whatever he wanted was fine.

Love didn't quite know what to expect when she entered the church, but she felt at home when she did. Nobody was judging or casting stones like she imagined they would; everyone was warm and welcoming. She kept going back to the church she visited with her friend, and she one day signed up for Bible study classes and volunteered for the women's missionary activities. Day after day, she grew stronger up to the point that she was able to let go of her grudge against the man who practically destroyed her life. She even learned and began to pray for him. The kids were fine, she was doing well at work, and she enrolled back into school for a higher degree. All these things wouldn't just fill the emptiness he created. How had something so exciting and promising come to this?

The melody of his voice which used to warm her, the aura of his body which made her heart race, and the touch of his hand which had always sent tingles down her spine were all gone. Dates were replaced with shifts at work, and drinking with friends was substituted for pizza and wine at home alone. They would pass each other in the streets like ghosts, neither of them with emotional reserves left to make a glorious glance at the other again. Life was becoming a monotony. The dreams they had have all died in the wind, and no energy of any kind was left to mend their brokenness.

Although she tried to forget the anguish she was really in when she was alone, the tears still flowed, often down to her already quivering lip. The comfort and touch of another person are what she urged to make her feel better. She spent idle moments thinking of alternatives that might provide a quick fix for her longing for another body on hers. She was mentally and emotionally crashing down, but a rebound partner was the last thing she needed, or so she thought.

Months later, Love reconnected with a childhood friend who swept her away with his charms, good looks, and even better manners. He was not the type of man she would have chosen for herself at first, but she was wiser now. She saw that he was a good man, he loved God, and most importantly, he completely adored her kids. He accepted Love for who she was and with all the baggage she came with. They began dating, and after a year, they began planning a wedding! To God be the glory!

Scripture Reflections

1. No matter the situation, you can bring it to God. He will always be willing to help. In Matthew 11:28,

   Come to me, all you who are weary and burdened, and I will give you rest.

2. God wants you to come to Him during the darkest of times, no matter what negative emotions you feel or the sins you have committed. He loves you endlessly and will lift you up if you let Him. In Psalm 37:17–19,

   For the power of the wicked will be broken, but the Lord upholds the righteous. The blameless spend their days under the Lord's care, and their inheritance will endure forever. In times of disaster, they will not wither; in days of famine they will enjoy plenty.

3. Take a moment to sit with God and ask Him for guidance. He will lead you toward positivity and grace. In Isaiah 58:11,

   The Lord will guide you always; he will satisfy your needs in a sun-scorched land and will strengthen your frame. You will be like a well-watered garden, like a spring whose waters never fail.

4. In 1 Corinthians 13:4–8,

   Love is patient, love is kind. It does not envy, it does not boast, it is not proud. It does not dishonor others, it is not self-seeking, it is not easily angered, it keeps no record of wrongs. Love does not delight in evil but rejoices with the truth. It always protects, always trusts, always hopes, always perseveres. Love never fails.

5. In 1 Thessalonians 5: 8,

   But since we belong to the day, let us be sober, putting on faith and love as a breastplate, and the hope of salvation as a helmet.

6. In 1 John 3: 18–20,

   Dear children, let us not love with words or speech but with actions and in truth. This is how we know that we belong to the truth and how we set our hearts at rest in his presence: If our hearts condemn us, we know that God is greater than our hearts, and he knows everything.

7. In Romans 12: 9–11,

   Love must be sincere. Hate what is evil; cling to what is good. Be devoted to one another in love. Honor one another above yourselves. Never be lacking in zeal, but keep your spiritual fervor, serving the Lord.

Let Us Pray

Dear Lord, Savior of the world, hear my cry. Just like Love in her story, I pray for Your love and Your protection. Help me remember that You made me in Your image and love me deeply. Help me to walk humbly with You. Allow me to learn from my past experiences. Not my will, Lord, but Yours be done! You are in control, and I trust that You have the final say. Enlighten my path so that I can see clearly where I'm going and where You want me to be. Hear me, O Lord! Arouse in me a hunger for You that grants me peace in my soul. Thank You for Your grace and Your mercy. In Jesus Christ's name, I pray, amen!

Notes

The Lord's Prayer

Our Father who art in heaven,
Hallowed be thy name.
Thy kingdom come.
Thy will be done,
on earth,
as it is in heaven.
Give us this day
our daily bread.
And forgive us our trespasses,
as we forgive those who trespass against us.
And lead us not into temptation,
but deliver us from evil:
For thine is the kingdom, the power, and the glory,
Forever and ever.
Amen.

About the Author

Yasmina Delacruz-Bailey was born and raised in New York City to Dominican Republic-descent parents. The youngest of seven and the only one born in the United States, Yasmina had the task of changing the narrative for her family and future generations. She took that task seriously and graduated top of her class at every level of her educational journey. While growing up in the South Bronx, she realized there was more out in the world for her. She wanted to be the best at everything she did. She graduated valedictorian of her high school class and later attained her bachelor's in business management and master's in human resources management. With a background in human resources and now a successful Realtor, Yasmina strives to be the best at helping and serving others, which has always been her passion. She is a faithful member of the Walters Memorial AME Zion Church in Bridgeport, Connecticut, and serves on the Christian education ministry, music ministry, praise and worship dance ministry, prayer ministry, and women's day ministry. Her dedication to her family, friends, and clients alike is an inspiration to many. She lives in Stratford, Connecticut, with her family and enjoys traveling with them.

Favorite scripture: Jeremiah 29:11, *"For I know the plans I have for you," declares the Lord, "plans to prosper you and not to harm you, plans to give you hope and a future."*

Printed in the USA
CPSIA information can be obtained
at www.ICGtesting.com
CBHW020410200424
6889CB00017B/10